King Edward III: A Retelling

David Bruce

Published by David Bruce, 2022.

KING EDWARD III: A RETELLING

First edition. July 8, 2022.

ISBN: 979-8201469252

Written by David Bruce.

Table of Contents

Dedication

Dedicated to My Brother Frank

Frank was reluctant to write the words below, but he did at my request because it's an opportunity to show that people still do good deeds. This can help restore people's faith in humanity.

"I've put some thought into this, and here a few Good Deeds I've done.

"I've bought breakfast more than once for complete strangers at my favorite local diner (Tommy's Diner) just because they looked like they could use a free meal.

"A woman came into Tommy's Diner, looking like she could use a decent meal and would appreciate it being free. I watched as she walked through the restaurant and sat down. I thought to myself, 'Buy her lunch.' I fought the urge and told myself no. I looked at her after she ordered and received her meal and thought to myself, 'Buy her lunch.' Again, I told myself no. She is a complete stranger, and money is hard to come by for me as well as everyone else. I was in line at the check-out waiting to pay my bill. She came up and got into line behind me and I thought to myself, 'Buy her lunch!' I looked at her, she looked at me, I reached out and grabbed her ticket, but she didn't want to let go. I told her sort of sternly, 'I don't know why, but I really, really want to pay for your lunch. I know we are complete strangers, but I feel like I am supposed to pay for your lunch. Will you please give me the pleasure of paying for this?' She almost cried, but she did allow me the pleasure.

"In Columbus, Ohio, almost always someone is at the gas station wanting money. One day this guy asked for money. I asked him, 'Why do you want money?' He said he's hungry. (If you don't know, Speedway has hotdogs and other food and drink items.) I said, 'Come inside, I'll buy you something to eat.' He was a really nice guy. His name was Dave, and he was an Army veteran; he may have been a little mentally ill after serving in the military. He talked to me about the war (don't know what war) and how he was over there fighting bulldozers. I think a couple of hotdogs and a hot coffee made his day. It really put a smile on his face. I ended up liking this guy and I'd look for him when I was getting gas so I could help him out.

"One time a guy came in the restaurant selling an old leather jacket for $10.00 so he could get some gas. It didn't fit me, and I didn't want it anyway, but I bought it and then donated the jacket.

"A woman was driving her car with the alarm going off, so I helped her figure out how to turn it off. She had the key fob, so I'm sure she didn't steal the car.

"These are a few of the good deeds I've had the pleasure of doing."
***

The doing of good deeds is important. As a free person, you can choose to live your life as a good person or as a bad person. To be a good person, do good deeds. To be a bad person, do bad deeds. If you do good deeds, you will become good. If you do bad deeds, you will become bad. To become the person you want to be, act as if you already are that kind of person. Each of us chooses what kind of person we will become. To become a good person, do the things a good person does. To become a bad person, do the things a bad person does. The opportunity to take action to become the kind of person you want to be is yours.

Human beings have free will. According to the Babylonian Niddah 16b, whenever a baby is to be conceived, the Lailah (angel in charge of contraception) takes the drop of semen that will result in the conception and asks God, "Sovereign of the Universe, what is going to be the fate of this drop? Will it develop into a robust or into a weak person? An intelligent or a stupid person? A wealthy or a poor person?" The Lailah asks all these questions, but it does not ask, "Will it develop into a righteous or a wicked person?" The answer to that question lies in the decisions to be freely made by the human being that is the result of the conception.

A Buddhist monk visiting a class wrote this on the chalkboard: "EVERYONE WANTS TO SAVE THE WORLD, BUT NO ONE WANTS TO HELP MOM DO THE DISHES." The students laughed, but the monk then said, "Statistically, it's highly unlikely that any of you will ever have the opportunity to run into a burning orphanage and rescue an infant. But, in the smallest gesture of kindness — a warm smile, holding the door for the person behind you, shoveling the driveway of the elderly person next door — you have committed an act of immeasurable profundity, because to each of us, our life is our universe."

In her book titled I HAVE CHOSEN TO STAY AND FIGHT, comedian Margaret Cho writes, "I believe that we get complimentary snack-size portions of the afterlife, and we all receive them in a different way." For Ms. Cho, many of her snack-size portions of the afterlife come in hip hop music. Other people get different snack-size portions of the afterlife, and we all must be on the lookout for them when they come our way. And perhaps doing good deeds and experiencing good deeds are snack-size portions of the afterlife.

Educate Yourself
Read Like a Wolf Eats
Be Excellent to Each Other
Books Then, Books Now, Books Forever

***

In this retelling, as in all my retellings, I have tried to make the work of literature accessible to modern readers who may lack some of the knowledge about mythology, religion, and history that the literary work's contemporary audience had.

Do you know a language other than English? If you do, I give you permission to translate this book, copyright your translation, publish or self-publish it, and keep all the royalties for yourself. (Do give me credit, of course, for the original retelling.)

I would like to see my retellings of classic literature used in schools, so I give permission to the country of Finland (and all other countries) to give copies of any or all of my retellings to all students forever. I also give permission to the state of Texas (and all other states) to give copies of this book to all students forever. I also give permission to all teachers to give copies of this book to all students forever.

Teachers need not actually teach my retellings. Teachers are welcome to give students copies of my eBooks as background material. For example, if they are teaching Homer's *Iliad* and *Odyssey*, teachers are welcome to give students copies of my *Virgil's* Aeneid: *A Retelling in Prose* and tell students, "Here's another ancient epic you may want to read in your spare time."

CAST OF CHARACTERS

THE ENGLISH
KING EDWARD III.
QUEEN Philippa, King Edward III's wife.
EDWARD THE BLACK PRINCE, Prince of Wales, their son [Edward Plantagenet; nicknamed Ned].
Earl of SALISBURY [William Montacute; Plantagenet].
COUNTESS of Salisbury, his wife.
EARL OF WARWICK, her father [Thomas de Beauchamp].
Sir William MONTAGUE, nephew of the Earl of Salisbury.
Earl of DERBY.
Lord AUDLEY.
Lord PERCY.
John COPLAND, esquire; later Sir John Copland.
LODOWICK, King Edward III's secretary.
FIRST ESQUIRE.
SECOND ESQUIRE.
A HERALD.
A MILITARY DRUMMER.
SUPPORTERS OF THE ENGLISH
Robert, COUNT OF ARTOIS, and Earl of Richmond.
LORD MOUNTFORT, Duke of Brittany.
GOBIN de Grace, a French prisoner.
THE FRENCH
KING JOHN II of FRANCE. The French called him **Jean** le Bon, which means "John the Good."
Prince CHARLES, Duke of Normandy, King John II's eldest son. He is the Dauphin (the oldest son, and heir apparent), and he will become King Charles V of France.
Prince PHILIP, King John II's youngest son. He will become Philip II, Duke of Burgundy.
DUKE OF LORRAINE, ambassador from France.
VILLIERS, a Lord.

CAPTAIN of Calais.

Another CAPTAIN (FRENCH CAPTAIN).

A MARINER.

FIRST FRENCH HERALD.

SECOND FRENCH HERALD.

THIRD FRENCH HERALD.

FIRST CITIZEN, from Crécy.

SECOND CITIZEN, from Crécy.

FIRST FRENCHMAN.

SECOND FRENCHMAN.

A WOMAN with two children.

Six WEALTHY CITIZENS of Calais.

Six POOR CITIZENS of Calais.

SUPPORTERS OF THE FRENCH

King of BOHEMIA.

POLISH CAPTAIN.

DANISH TROOPS.

THE SCOTS

KING DAVID Bruce of Scotland. He is King David II.

Sir William DOUGLAS.

FIRST MESSENGER.

SECOND MESSENGER.

NOTA BENE

In 1308, Isabella, daughter of King Philip IV of France, married King Edward II of England.

In 1312, King Edward III of England was born.

King Edward III of England reigned from 25 January 1327 – 21 June 1377.

The Battle of Crécy was fought on 26 August 1346.

The Battle of Poitiers was fought on 19 September 1356.

We don't read Elizabethan plays to learn history:

• This play has a reference to King John II of France being "three degrees removed" from King Charles IV of France. Actually, that is true of Philip of Valois, who became King Philip VI of France (reigned 1328 – 1350). King John II reigned from 22 August 1350 – 8 April 1364.

• The Battle of Crécy and the Battle of Poitiers were fought ten years apart, but in this play, the two battles are fought close together in time. Such telescoping of time is common in Elizabethan history plays.

CHAPTER 1

— 1.1 —

[Scene 1]

King Edward III, the Earl of Derby, Edward the Black Prince, Lord Audley, the Earl of Warwick, and the Count of Artois talked together.

King Edward III said, "Count Robert of Artois, although you are banished from France, your native country, yet with us you shall retain as great a seigniory, aka domain, for we make you the Earl of Richmond here."

Using the royal plural, he added, "Now continue to tell us our pedigree. Who next succeeded Philip le Beau?"

Philip le Beau was Philip the Fair, who had ruled as King Philip IV of France.

The Count of Artois answered, "Three sons of his, who all successively sat upon their father's regal throne, yet died and left no issue of their loins. None of those three sons left any children."

"But was my mother — Isabella — sister to those three men?" King Edward III asked.

"She was, my lord," the Count of Artois answered, "and Isabella was the only daughter that this Philip had. Your father took Isabella as his wife; and from the fragrant garden of her womb your gracious self, the flower of Europe's hope, was born. Because of this genealogy, you are the inheritor to France.

"But note the rancor of rebellious minds: When thus the male lineage of Philip le Beau was out, the French obscured your mother's privilege, and although she was the next in blood lineage, the French proclaimed John of the house of Valois their King now: King John II.

"The reason was this: They say the realm of France, replete with princes of great parentage, ought not to allow a governor to rule France unless he has been descended of the male line, and that's the particular ground of their contempt with which they strive to exclude your grace from the French throne."

King Philip III of France fathered King Philip IV of France, who fathered Isabella, who lived the longest of King Philip IV's four children. If females could inherit the throne, she would have inherited it.

Isabella married King Edward II of England, and they became the parents of King Edward III of England, and so Edward III of England is directly descended from King Philip III of France through the female line.

The French, however, did not recognize kingly succession through the female line. Nevertheless, King Edward III of England regarded himself as the rightful King of France.

King Edward III said, "But they shall find that forged ground of theirs consists only of dusty heaps of brittle sand."

The Count of Artois said, "Perhaps it will be thought a heinous thing that I, a Frenchman, should say what I have told you, but I call on Heaven to witness my vows: It is not hate nor any private wrong, but love for my country and for what is right that provokes my tongue to be thus lavish in report.

"You are the lineally descended watchman of our peace, and John of Valois — the so-called King John II of France — indirectly has climbed to the throne: His lineal descent from King Philip II is not direct, as is yours.

"What then should subjects do but embrace their King?

"Yes, and wherein may our duty be seen more than in striving to repress a tyrant's pride and to place the true shepherd of our commonwealth on his rightful throne?"

King Edward III said, "This counsel, Count of Artois, similar to fruitful showers, has added growth to my dignity; and by the fiery vigor of your words, hot courage is engendered in my breast, which heretofore was racked in ignorance, but now mounts with golden wings of fame and will confirm beautiful Isabella's descent, and will yoke with steel the stubborn necks of those who kick against and resist my sovereignty in France."

A horn sounded.

"It is a messenger," King Edward III said.

He ordered, "Lord Audley, find out from where the messenger is coming."

Lord Audley exited and immediately returned and said, "The Duke of Lorraine, having crossed the seas, asks that he may have conversation with your highness."

King Edward III ordered, "Admit him, lords, so that we may hear his news."

Lord Audley opened the door and admitted the messenger — the Duke of Lorraine, who was serving as ambassador to King John II of France.

King Edward III said, "Say, Duke of Lorraine, for what reason you have come here."

The Duke of Lorraine answered, "The most renowned King John II of France greets you, King Edward III of England, and by me commands that because the Guienne dukedom has been bestowed on you as his liberal gift, you do him lowly homage for that dukedom.

"And for that purpose here I summon you to go to France within these forty days, so that there, in accordance with the custom, you may be sworn to be a true liegeman to our King, or else your title in that province dies, and he himself will possess again the dukedom."

"See how opportunity laughs in the face at me," King Edward III said. "No sooner am I minded to prepare for France, but immediately I am invited to come there — indeed, with threats of a penalty I am urged to come to France! It would be childish of me to tell him no.

"Duke of Lorraine, return this answer to your lord:

"I mean to visit him as he requests, but how? Not servilely disposed to bend my knee to him, but like a conqueror to make him bow his knee to me. His lame unpolished tricks have come to light, and truth has pulled the mask from his face — the mask that set a deceptive appearance upon his arrogance.

"Dare he command me to give him an oath of loyalty and allegiance? Tell him the crown that he usurps is mine, and where he sets his foot he ought to kneel to me.

"It is not a petty dukedom that I claim, but all the dominions of the realm of France, which if with grudging he refuse to yield to me, I'll take away those borrowed plumes of his and send him naked to the wilderness."

The Duke of Lorraine replied, "Then, Edward III, here in spite of all your lords, I pronounce defiance to your face."

King Edward III's son, Edward the Black Prince, said, "Defiance, Frenchman? We rebound defiance back, even to the bottom of your master's throat; and let it be spoken with reverence of King Edward III, who is my gracious father, and these other lords, that I regard your message to be only scurrilous, and I regard him who sent you to be like the lazy drone that has crept up by stealth to the eagle's nest, from whence we'll shake him with so rough a storm as others shall be warned by his harm."

A drone is a male honeybee that does no work but exists in order to impregnate the Queen bee.

Edward the Black Prince may have had in mind Aesop's fable about the beetle and the eagle. A hare asked a beetle to protect her from an eagle, and the beetle asked the eagle to spare the hare, but the eagle killed the hare in front of the beetle. To get revenge, the beetle climbed to the eagle's nest and pushed the eagle's eggs out of the nest, destroying its progeny. If Edward the Black Prince had this fable in mind, he had created a different ending to the story: The eagle knocked the intruder out of the nest.

The Earl of Warwick said, "Bid him leave off the lion's skin he wears lest, meeting with the lion in the field, the real lion tears him to pieces for his pride."

He was alluding to another of Aesop's fables: An ass came across a lion's skin and wore it. The other animals saw the lion's skin and were afraid until the ass brayed. The Earl of Warwick had changed the fable and given it another ending: The donkey then came across a live lion that killed it. Of course, this was an analogy: The lion was the English army, and the field was a battlefield.

The Count of Artois, who was a Frenchman, said, "The soundest counsel I can give his grace John II is to surrender before he is forced to surrender. A voluntary mischief has less scorn than when reproach with violence is born."

He meant that it is better to voluntarily confess to having made a mistake than to be forced to suffer rebuke and punishment.

The Duke of Lorraine said, "Degenerate traitor, viper to the place where you were fostered in your infancy! Do you have a part in this conspiracy?"

Of course, the Duke of Lorraine regarded the Count of Artois as a traitor to France, and so he compared him to a viper, which this culture believed to bite its way out of its mother at birth. According to the Duke of Lorraine, the Count of Artois ought to be loyal to France, which had nurtured him.

This culture regarded vipers as betrayers. Another of Aesop's fables was about a farmer who found a frozen viper. Taking pity on it, he put it in his jacket to warm it up. Once the viper had warmed up, it bit the farmer.

The Duke of Lorraine drew his sword.

King Edward III drew his own sword and said, "Duke of Lorraine, behold the sharpness of this steel. Fervent desire that sits against my heart is far more thorny-pricking than this blade, so that with the nightingale I shall be scarred as often as I dispose myself to rest until my colors — my battle standards — are displayed in France."

This culture believed that the nightingale pushed its breast against a sharp thorn as it sang.

King Edward III continued, "This is your final answer, so be gone."

The Duke of Lorraine replied, "Neither your answer nor any English boast or bravado afflicts me as much as does this Frenchman's poisoned view: That is most false, although it should most of all be true."

In other words, what bothered him was not a sword or a threat or a boast, but the disloyalty of his fellow Frenchman, who was a traitor although he should have been a loyal Frenchman.

The Duke of Lorraine exited, and King Edward III sheathed his sword.

King Edward III said, referring to God, "Now, Lord, our swift-moving ship is under sail, our gage is thrown, and war is soon begun, but not so quickly brought to an end."

A gage is figuratively a challenge; literally, it is a gauntlet or glove thrown down as a challenge.

Sir William Montague entered the room.

Seeing him, King Edward III said, "But why is Sir William Montague coming here?"

He then asked him, "How stands the league between the Scot and us?"

Sir William Montague replied, "Cracked and broken, my renowned lord: The treacherous King David II of Scotland no sooner was informed of your withdrawing your army back from the Scottish border, but immediately forgetting his former oath of peace, he invaded the towns on the border. Berwick has been defeated, Newcastle has been spoiled and lost, and now the tyrant has surrounded with siege the castle of Roxborough, where the Countess of Salisbury, who is in the castle, is likely to perish."

King Edward III said, "The Countess of Salisbury is your daughter, Earl of Warwick, isn't she? Hasn't her husband served very long in Bretagne about establishing Lord Mountfort there?"

"She is my daughter, my lord," the Earl of Warwick replied.

King Edward III said, "Ignoble David II, have you no one other than defenseless ladies to grieve with your threatening weapons? But I will make you shrink your snail-like horns!"

Snails have "horns" — actually, they are tentacles — that pull back when touched.

King Edward III ordered, "First, therefore, Lord Audley, this shall be your responsibility: Go and levy foot-soldiers for our wars in France.

"And, Ned the Black Prince, take muster of our men at arms. In every shire draft a separate band of foot soldiers. Let them be soldiers of a lusty spirit such as dread nothing except the blot of dishonor. Be wary, therefore, since we are commencing a renown-bringing war with so mighty a nation.

"Earl of Derby, be the ambassador for us to our father-in-law, the Earl of Hainault. Make him acquainted with our enterprise, and likewise order him with our own allies who are in Flanders to solicit also the Emperor of Almagne in our name.

"I myself, while all of you are jointly thus employed, will, with these forces whom I have at hand, march and once more repulse the traitorous Scottish King.

"But, sirs, be resolute. We shall have wars on every side; and Ned, you must begin now to forget your study and your books, and inure your shoulders to the weight of armor."

Edward the Black Prince replied, "As cheerful sounding to my youthful spirits is this tumult of war's increasing broils, as at the coronation of a King, the joyful clamors of the people are when they pronounce '*Ave Caesar*' aloud."

Ave Caesar means, "Hail, Caesar."

He continued, "Within this school of honor, I shall learn either to sacrifice my foes to death, or in a rightful quarrel spend my breath. Then cheerfully let us each go forward in our separate ways; in great affairs it is wrong to engage in delay."

— 1.2 —

[Scene 2]

The Countess of Salisbury, who was standing on the battlements of the castle of Roxborough, said to herself, "Alas, how much in vain my poor eyes gaze, looking for the succor that my sovereign, King Edward III, should send."

She then spoke in an apostrophe to Sir William Montague, who was not present because he had gone to King Edward III to ask for aid:

"Ah, Sir William Montague, my nephew, I fear you lack the lively spirit needed to sharply solicit with vehement suit the King in my behalf. You do not tell him what a grief it is to be the scorned captive to a Scot, either to be wooed with broad untuned oaths, or forced by rough insulting barbarism."

The word "forced" means "raped."

She continued, "You do not tell him, if King David II of Scotland prevails here, how much the Scots will deride us in the North, and, in their vile uncivilized skipping jigs, bray forth their conquest and our overthrow, even in the barren, bleak, and fruitless air."

King David II of Scotland, Sir William Douglas, and the Duke of Lorraine, who was the French ambassador, arrived. They stood below the battlement on which the Countess of Salisbury was standing.

Unseen, the Countess of Salisbury said, "I must withdraw. The everlasting foe comes to the wall; I'll secretly step aside and listen to their babble, which is blunt, obtuse, and full of pride."

King David II said, "My lord of Lorraine, commend us to our brother King John II of France, as he is the man in Christendom whom we most reverence and entirely love.

"Concerning your embassy to us, return to France and say that we with England will not enter parley, nor will we ever make fair weather or make a truce, but instead we will burn their towns neighboring us and so persist with eager inroads beyond their city of York. And never shall our bonny riders rest, nor will the canker of rust have the time to eat their light-borne bridle bits or their nimble spurs, nor lay aside their jackets of linked mail, nor hang their staves of grained Scottish ash peacefully upon their city walls, nor from their buttoned tawny leather belts dismiss their biting short swords, until your King John II cries out, 'Enough, spare England now for pity!'

"Farewell, and tell him that you leave us here before this castle; say you came from us exactly at the time when we had that yielded to our hands."

The Duke of Lorraine replied, "I take my leave and fairly will return your gratifying greeting to my King."

The Duke of Lorraine exited.

King David II said, "Now, Sir William Douglas, let us return again to our former task: the division of the spoils that are certain to be ours."

"My liege, I request the lady and no more," Sir William Douglas said. He meant the Countess of Salisbury.

King David II replied, "Quiet, sir, first I must make my choice, and first I do reserve her for myself."

"Why then, my liege, let me enjoy her jewels," Sir William Douglas said.

King David II said, "Those jewels are her own property, still belonging to her, and who inherits her has those jewels with all the rest she has."

A Scottish messenger hastily arrived and ran over to King David II and said, "My liege, as we were spurring our horses on the hills to fetch in booty, marching hitherward we were able to see a mighty army of men. The sun reflecting on the armor showed a field of plate armor, a wood of wooden pikes advancing.

"Your highness must speedily make a decision concerning this. An easy march within four hours will bring the hindmost ranks of the enemy to this place, my liege."

Panicked, King David II cried, "Retreat! Retreat! It is King Edward III of England!"

"Jemmy, my man, saddle my bonny black," Sir William Douglas ordered.

"Do you intend to fight, Douglas?" King David II said. "We are too weak."

"I know it well, my liege, and therefore I will flee," Sir William Douglas said.

The Countess of Salisbury revealed herself and said, "My lords of Scotland, will you stay and have a drink?"

"She mocks us, Douglas," King David II said. "I cannot endure it."

"Tell me, my good lord, who is he who must have the lady, and who is he who must have her jewels?" the Countess of Salisbury said. "I am sure, my lords, you will not leave here until after you have shared the spoils."

King David II said, "She heard the messenger and she heard our talk, and now that comfort makes her scorn us."

Another Scottish messenger arrived and said, "Arm yourself, my good lord. Oh, we are all unexpectedly attacked!"

The Countess of Salisbury said to the Scottish King, "Ride after the French ambassador, my liege, and tell him that you dare not ride to York. Give as your excuse that your bonny horse is lame."

King David II said, "She heard that, too! This is intolerable grief!"

He then said, "Woman, farewell. Although I do not stay —"

The Scots exited.

The Countess of Salisbury finished King David II's statement for him: "'— it is not because of fear' — and yet you run away."

She continued, "Oh, happy comfort, welcome to our house! The confident, boisterous, and boasting Scottish King, who swore before my walls he would not retreat for all the armed power of this land, with faceless fear that always turns its back, has turned away from here and is now facing the blasting north-east wind upon the mere report and name of arms."

Sir William Montague arrived.

Seeing him, the Countess of Salisbury said, "Oh, summer's day, see where my nephew comes!"

"How fares my aunt?" Sir William Montague asked her. "We are not Scots, so why do you shut your gates against your friends?"

The Countess of Salisbury said, "Well may I give a welcome, nephew, to you, for you come well — at a good time — to chase my foes away from here."

"King Edward III himself is coming in person here," Sir William Montague said. "Dear aunt, descend and welcome his highness."

The Countess of Salisbury asked, "How may I entertain his majesty in such a way as to show my duty and his dignity?"

She descended from the battlement.

King Edward III, the Earl of Warwick, the Count of Artois, and others arrived. The Earl of Warwick was the father of the Countess of Salisbury.

King Edward III asked, "Have the stealing foxes fled and gone before we could release our dogs to bite at their heels?"

Earl of Warwick replied, "They have fled, my liege, but with a cheerful cry hot and hardy hounds chase them at the heels."

The Countess of Salisbury walked out of the castle to greet King Edward III.

"This is the Countess, isn't it, Earl of Warwick?" King Edward III asked, seeing her coming.

The Earl of Warwick replied, "Yes, this is she, my liege, whose beauty the fear of tyrants has sullied, withered, overcast, and destroyed just as pernicious winds do to a May blossom."

King Edward III asked, "Has she been more beautiful, Earl of Warwick, than she is now?"

The Earl of Warwick answered, "My gracious King, she is not at all beautiful now in comparison with her former self. If her beautiful former self could be present for comparison now, you would see that her present self is stained."

King Edward III said to himself, "What strange enchantment lurked in those her eyes when they excelled this excellence they have, when now her dim decline has power to draw my subject eyes from piercing majesty to gaze on her with doting admiration?"

King Edward III was like a sun at high noon, while the Countess, if what her father had said was true, was like a setting sun in comparison with when her beauty was at its height, yet the Countess' setting sun was enough to outshine the King's noon sun and make him her subject.

The Countess of Salisbury knelt and said, "In duty lower than the ground I kneel, and in addition to my dull, unfeeling knees, I bow my feeling heart to witness my obedience to your highness with many millions of a subject's thanks for this your royal presence, whose approach has driven war and danger away from my gate."

King Edward III said, "Lady, stand up, I come to bring you peace, although thereby I have purchased war."

His words had a double meaning: 1) He had come to bring her peace, and by so doing he had purchased war with the Scots, and 2) He had come to bring her peace, and by so doing he had purchased war with his emotions — although he was married, he was attracted to her.

The Countess of Salisbury said, "No war to you, my liege; the Scots are gone, and they gallop home toward Scotland with their hate."

King Edward III thought, *Lest yielding here I pine in shameful love —*

He then said out loud, "— come, we'll pursue the Scots. Count of Artois, let's go."

The Countess of Salisbury said, "Stay a little while, my gracious sovereign, and let the power of a mighty King honor our roof; my husband in the wars, when he shall hear about it, will triumph for joy. So then, my dear liege, now do not hoard your state — since you are here at the wall, enter our homely gate."

King Edward III replied, "Pardon me, Countess, I will come no nearer. I dreamed last night of treason, and I fear."

The Countess of Salisbury said, "Far from this place let ugly treason lie."

King Edward III thought, *No farther off than her conspiring eye, which shoots infected poison in my heart beyond repulse of intelligence or cure of art. Now in the sun alone it does not lie with light to take light from a mortal eye, for here two day-stars — her eyes — that my eyes would see more than the sun steal my own light from me. Contemplative desire, desire to be in contemplation that may master you.*

The sun can dazzle the King with its light; now he knows that the Countess' eyes can also dazzle him with their light. Her eyes are like conspirators that infect his heart with poison — the poison of love — that he cannot cure.

King Edward II ordered, "Earl of Warwick, Count of Artois, let's get on horseback and ride away."

"What can I say to make my sovereign stay?" the Countess of Salisbury asked.

King Edward III thought, *Why does she need a tongue when her speaking eye is more persuasive than winning oratory?*

The Countess of Salisbury continued, "Let not your presence, like the April sun, flatter our earth and suddenly be done. Do not make the outward wall of the castle happier than you will grace our inner house.

"Our house, my liege, is like a country swain whose rude clothing and blunt and plain manners foretell nothing good, yet the country swain is inwardly beautified with bounty's riches and with fair hidden pride.

"For where the golden ore buried lies, the ground above it that is unadorned with nature's tapestry of vegetation seems barren, sere, infertile, fruitless, and dry.

"And where the upper turf of earth boasts its splendor, perfumes, and variegated richness, if you delve there under the surface, you will find that this splendor and richness spring from ordure and dung and the side of a decaying corpse.

"But to conclude my all too long comparison, these ragged outer walls of my castle are no testimony to what is within, for they are similar to a cloak that hides from the waste of weather the magnificence that is underneath.

"Be more gracious than my terms can entreat you to be, and entreat yourself to stay a while with me."

King Edward III thought, *She is as wise as she is beautiful — when wisdom keeps the gate as beauty's guard, what a passionate fit can be heard!*

He said out loud, "Countess, although my business urges me onward, it shall attend while I attend on you."

The first "attend" meant "wait"; the second "attend" ("attend on") meant "visit."

The King added, "Come on, my lords, here I will lodge tonight."

CHAPTER 2
— 2.1 —
[Scene 3]

Lodowick, King Edward III's secretary, said this to himself about the King's falling in love with the Countess of Salisbury:

"I might perceive his eye in her eye to be lost, his ear to drink her sweet tongue's utterance, and his changing passions, like inconstant clouds that move forcefully upon the carriage of the winds, to increase and die, wax and wane, in his disturbed cheeks.

"Lo, when she blushed, even then he looked pale, as if her cheeks by some enchanted power had attracted the cherry blood from his cheeks. Soon, with reverent fear when she grew pale, his cheeks put on their scarlet ornaments, but they were no more like her radiant red than brick is to coral, or live things are to dead.

"Why did he then thus copy her looks? If she blushed, it was from tender modest shame because of being in the sacred presence of a King.

"If he blushed, it was from red immodest shame to lower his eyes improperly as if in submission — he is a King and he ought not to do that. No King should lower himself and submit to a subject.

"If she looked pale, it was a weak woman's fear of being in the presence of a King.

"If he looked pale, it was with guilty fear to dote wrongly on her — he is a mighty King and he ought not to do that.

"So then, Scottish wars, farewell. I fear the war will prove to be a lingering English siege of silly, foolish, obstinate love."

Seeing the King coming, he said to himself, "Here comes his highness walking all alone."

King Edward III said this to himself about the Countess of Salisbury:

"She has grown far more fairer since I came hither. Her voice is every word more silvery than the previous word. Her intelligent conversation is more fluent. What a strange discourse she unfolded about King David II and his

Scots! 'Even thus,' said she, 'he said' — and then she spoke broadly, with the epithets and accents of the Scot, but somewhat better than the Scot could speak. 'And thus spoke she' — and answered the question then herself, for who could speak like her?"

In entertaining King Edward III with an account of what she had heard King David II of Scotland say and of how she had spoken to him, she had taken on the roles of both King David II and herself.

King Edward III continued, "But she herself breathes from the wall an angel from Heaven's note of sweet defiance to her barbarous foes. When she would talk of peace, I think her tongue commanded war to go to prison; when she spoke of war, it awakened Caesar from his Roman grave so he could hear war beautified by her discourse.

"Wisdom is foolishness except in her tongue. Beauty is a slander except in her fair face. There is no summer except in her cheerful looks, and there is no frosty winter except in her disdain.

"I cannot blame the Scots who besieged her, for she is all the treasure of our land, but I call them cowards because they ran away despite having so rich and fair a reason to stay."

He then called, "Are you there, Lodowick? Give me ink and paper."

"I will, my liege," Lodowick replied.

Using the royal plural, King Edward III added, "And tell the lords to carry on with their play at chess, for we will walk and meditate alone."

"I will, my sovereign," Lodowick replied.

He exited to carry out his orders.

King Edward III said to himself about Lodowick, "This fellow is well read in poetry, and he has a vigorous and persuasive spirit. I will acquaint him with my passion for the Countess of Salisbury, which he shall shadow with a veil of fine fabric through which the Queen of Beauty's Queen shall see that she herself is the cause of my infirmity."

Beauty's Queen is the goddess Venus, but the Countess of Salisbury was more beautiful than Venus in the eyes of King Edward III and therefore he regarded the Countess of Salisbury as the Queen of Beauty's Queen.

Seeing Lodowick returning, he asked, "Have you pen, ink, and paper ready, Lodowick?"

"They are ready, my liege," Lodowick replied.

King Edward III said, "Then in the summer arbor — this shady tree bower — sit by me."

Using the royal plural, he said, "We will make it our council house or private apartment. Since green — new and spring-like — are our thoughts, green will be the meeting place where we will ease ourself by unburdening them.

"Now, Lodowick, invoke some golden muse to bring you here an enchanted pen."

Ancient poets would create an invocation to a muse to ask for help in telling a story.

King Edward III continued, "Ask for an enchanted pen that may for sighs set down true sighs indeed. When talking of grief, the enchanted pen will make you readily groan. And when you write about tears, embed the word 'tears' before and after with such sweet laments that it may raise drops in a Tartar's eye, and make a flint-heart Scythian full of pity — for so much moving has a poet's pen."

This society regarded the Tartars and the Scythians as pitiless.

King Edward III continued, "Then if you are a poet, move yourself so, and be enriched by your sovereign's love, for if the touch of sweet concordant strings could force the ears of Hell to pay attention, how much more shall the strains of poets' intelligence beguile and ravish soft and humane minds?"

Orpheus was an ancient musician who went to the Land of the Dead and played so beautifully that Hades, god of the underworld, made an agreement for Orpheus to return his late wife to the Land of the Living.

Lodowick asked, "To whom, my lord, shall I direct my style?"

King Edward III replied, "To one who shames the fair and makes foolish the wise, whose body is an abstract or a summary that contains each general virtue in the world.

"'Better than beautiful' you must begin. Devise for 'fair' a fairer word than 'fair,' and every special physical and intellectual quality that you would praise, fly it a pitch above the soar of praise."

The pitch of a hawk is the height to which a bird of prey flies before swooping.

King Edward III continued, "Don't be afraid of being convicted of flattery, for if your admiration were ten times more than what you will write, the merit of what you are to praise exceeds that by ten times ten thousand.

"Begin — I intend to contemplate while you write. Don't forget to set down how passionate, how heartsick, and how full of languishment her beauty makes me."

Lodowick asked, "Am I writing to a woman?"

King Edward III asked, "What other beauty could triumph over me, and who except women do our love-songs greet? Did you think that I ordered you to praise a horse?"

"It is necessary that I know what social rank she is or what status she has, my lord," Lodowick replied.

King Edward III replied, "She is of such estate that hers is like a throne, and my estate is like the footstool where she treads. Knowing that, you may judge what her condition is by the proportion of her mightiness.

"Write on, while I peruse her in my thoughts."

He then said this to himself about the Countess of Salisbury:

"Should I compare her voice to music or the nightingale? To music every summer-leaping country lover compares his sunburnt lover when she speaks, and why should I speak of the nightingale?"

"Summer-leaping" can mean leaping in the enjoyment of the good weather that comes in summer, but the word "leaping" is also used to describe male animals mounting female animals.

King Edward III continued, "The nightingale sings of adulterous wrong."

In myth, Tereus, who was Philomela's sister's husband, raped Philomela. To prevent Philomela from telling anyone about the rape, he cut out her tongue. Philomela, however, wove a tapestry that told about the rape. When Procne, her sister, saw the tapestry and realized what had happened, she killed her son and fed him to Tereus, the father. When he realized what had happened, he pursued Philomela and Procne, intending to kill them, but they prayed to the gods for help. The gods transformed Philomela into a nightingale, Procne into a swallow, and Tereus into a hoopoe.

King Edward III continued, "The nightingale's singing about adulterous wrong, compared to my adulterous love for the Countess, is too satirical, for in my case sin, although sin, would not be so esteemed, but rather virtue sin, sin virtue deemed."

He was married, but he was pursuing the Countess of Salisbury with his adulterous love. Because the Countess was so excellent, he believed that it was not a sin to pursue her, but rather it was a virtue; the sin would lie in not pursuing her.

King Edward III continued, "Her hair is far softer than the silkworm's twist, similar to a flattering mirror that makes more beautiful the yellow amber of her hair — 'similar to a flattering mirror' I mention too soon; for when writing about her eyes, I'll say that like a mirror they catch the sun, and the hot reflection rebounds from the mirror against my breast and burns my heart within.

"Ah, what a world of melodious accompaniment my soul makes upon this spontaneous foundation of love!"

He then said out loud, "Come, Lodowick, have you turned your ink into gold? If not, simply write in capital letters my mistress' name and it will gild your paper."

Some books of the time were decorated with capital letters made with gold leaf.

King Edward III continued, "Read, Lodowick, read. Fill the empty hollows of my ears with the sweet hearing of your poetry."

Lodowick said, "I have not yet finished praising her."

King Edward III said, "Her praise is like my love, both are infinite, and they apprehend such violent extremes that they disdain an ending period. Her beauty has no match but my affection. Her beauty is more than most, and my affection is most, and more than more.

"To praise her beauty adequately is harder than to count the drops of water in the sea, or to count the mass of sand-sized particles of the earth as they drop, grain by grain, in an immense hourglass and to memorize each sand-sized particle.

"So then why do you talk about an end to that which craves unending admiration? There can be no end to praising her beauty.

"Read what you have written; let us hear it."

Lodowick read the first line:

"More fair and chaste than is the Queen of shades —"

King Edward III interrupted, "That line has two faults that are gross and palpable."

Readers may be forgiven for thinking that the "Queen of shades" was Proserpina (Greek name: Persephone), wife of Hades, god of the Underworld, where resides the shades of the dead, but King Edward III believed that the phrase referred to Diana (Greek name: Artemis) the moon goddess.

King Edward III continued, "Do you compare her to the pale Queen of night, who being set in dark seems therefore light?"

The moon appears light because it is set against the dark night sky.

He continued, "What is she — the moon — when the sun lifts up its head, but like a fading candle, dim and dead? My love shall challenge the eye — the sun — of Heaven at noon, and, when she takes off her mask, she shall outshine the golden sun."

Women in this culture wore masks to protect their faces from the sun.

Lodowick asked, "What is the other fault, my sovereign lord?"

King Edward III ordered, "Read over the line again."

Lodowick began, "'*More fair and chaste*' — "

Again, King Edward III interrupted, "I did not ask you to talk of chastity, to investigate in such detail the treasure of her mind, for I had rather have her chased than chaste."

Horny men often regard chastity as a vice, not a virtue. Readers should note that Diana is the goddess of chastity.

He continued, "Out with the moon line, I will have none of it, and let me have her likened to the sun: Say that she has thrice more splendor than the sun, that her perfections emulate the sun, that she breeds sweet flowers as plenteous as the sun, that she thaws cold winter like the sun, that she gladdens fresh summer like the sun, that she dazzles gazers like the sun, and in this application to the sun, tell her to be as free and open to all as the sun, which smiles upon the basest weed as lovingly as on the fragrant rose.

"Let's see what follows that same moonlight line."

Lodowick read what he had written:

"'*More fair and chaste than is the Queen of shades,*

"'*More bold in constancy*' —"

King Edward III asked, "In constancy than who?

Lodowick read, "'*Than Judith was.*'"

Judith 13:6-10 (Douay-Rheims 1899 American Edition) tells the story of how the Jewish widow Judith decapitated the enemy general Holofernes:

6 And Judith stood before the bed praying with tears, and the motion of her lips in silence,

7 Saying: Strengthen me, O Lord God of Israel, and in this hour look on the works of my hands, that as thou hast promised, thou mayst raise up Jerusalem thy city: and that I may bring to pass that which I have purposed, having a belief that it might be done by thee.

8 And when she had said this, she went to the pillar that was at his bed's head, and loosed his sword that hung tied upon it.

9 And when she had drawn it out, she took him by the hair of his head, and said: Strengthen me, O Lord God, at this hour.

10 And she struck twice upon his neck, and cut off his head, and took off his canopy from the pillars, and rolled away his headless body.

Judith was loyal to her God; she saved the Israelites by decapitating the general of their enemy as he lay in a drunken stupor. Although many men courted her, she remained an unmarried widow for the rest of the life.

By seeking to commit adultery, King Edward III was not loyal to his God.

King Edward III said, "Oh, monstrous line! Put a sword in the next line, and I shall woo her and ask her to cut off my head! Blot, blot out that line, good Lodowick; let us hear the next line."

Lodowick said, "That's all that I have written so far."

King Edward III said, "I thank you then because you have done little ill, but what little is done is surpassing, surpassing ill. No, let the Captain talk about boisterous war, and let the prisoner talk about his enclosed dark constraint. The sick man best sets down the pangs of death, the starving man best sets down the sweetness of a feast, the frozen soul best sets down the benefit of fire, and every man suffering a grief best sets down his happy opposite. Love cannot sound well except in lovers' tongues. Give me the pen and paper; I will write."

The Countess of Salisbury appeared and walked over to them, and King Edward III pretended that he and Lodowick had been talking about military matters.

He said quietly to Lodowick, "Quiet, here comes the treasurer of my spirit!"

He then said loudly, "Lodowick, you don't know how to deploy the ranks of soldiers."

Pointing to the paper, he said, "These wings, these flankers, and these squadrons argue that you are deficient in military training. You should have placed this one here, this other one over here."

The Countess of Salisbury said, "Pardon my boldness, my thrice gracious lords. Let my intrusion here be called my duty that comes to see how my sovereign fares."

King Edward III said to Lodowick, "Go, and deploy them in what form I have told you."

The Countess of Salisbury understood King Edward III to be referring to ranks of soldiers, but Lodowick understood him to be referring to ranks of words.

Lodowick said, "I go."

He exited.

The Countess of Salisbury said, "I am sorry to see my liege so sad. What may your subject do to drive away from you your gloomy consort, which is sullen melancholy?"

"Ah, lady," King Edward III said, "I am blunt and cannot strew the flowers of solace on a ground of shame. Since I came hither, Countess, I am wronged."

The Countess of Salisbury said, "May God forbid that anyone in my house should think to wrong my sovereign! Thrice gentle King, acquaint me with the cause of your discontent."

"How near then shall I be to a remedy?" King Edward III asked.

"As near, my liege, as all my woman's power can pawn itself to buy your remedy," the Countess of Salisbury said.

"If you are speaking the truth," King Edward III said, "then I will have my redress. Engage your power to redeem my joys, and I will be joyful, Countess, or else I will die."

"I will, my liege," she replied.

King Edward III said, "Swear, Countess, that you will."

"I swear by Heaven, I will," the Countess of Salisbury said.

King Edward III said, "Then take yourself a little way aside, and tell yourself that a King dotes on you. Say that it is within your power to make him happy, and that you have sworn to give him all the joy it is within your power to give. Do this and tell me when I shall be happy."

The Countess of Salisbury replied, "All this is done, my thrice dread sovereign. That power of love that I have power to give, you have with all my devout obedience. Employ me how you will to test what I told you."

"You heard me say that I dote on you," King Edward III said.

The Countess of Salisbury replied, "If you dote on my beauty, take it if you can. Although my beauty is little, I prize it ten times less. If you dote on my virtue, take it if you can, for giving increases the amount of virtue one has. Dote on whatever you can that I can give to you, and you can take it away, and have it."

"It is your beauty that I would enjoy," King Edward III said.

"Oh, if my beauty were painted on my face, I would wipe it off and dispossess myself of it so I could give it to you, but sovereign, it is soldered to my life. Take one and you take both, for like a humble shadow it haunts the sunshine of my summer's life."

King Edward III said, "But you may allow me to sexually sport with it."

The Countess of Salisbury, who was married to her still-living husband, the Earl of Salisbury, said, "As easily may my intellectual soul be lent away and yet my body live, as I could lend my body, which is the palace to my soul, away from my soul and yet retain my soul.

"My body is my soul's bower, my soul's court, my soul's abbey, and my soul is an angel pure, divine, and unspotted with sin. If I should lend my soul's house, my lord, to you, I would kill my poor soul and the death of my poor soul would kill me."

King Edward III asked, "Didn't you swear to give me what I wanted?"

"I did, my liege," the Countess of Salisbury said, "as long as what you want, I could give to you. You are asking for something I cannot give to you."

King Edward III said, "I wish no more of you than you may give, and I do not beg but rather buy — that is, I buy your love, and for that love of yours in rich exchange I give to you my love."

Knowing that King Edward III was also married, the Countess of Salisbury said, "Except that your lips are sacred, my lord, you would profane the holy name of love. That love you offer me you cannot give, for Caesar owes that tribute to his Queen. That love you beg of me I cannot give, for Sarah owes that duty to her lord."

This part of 1 Peter 3:6 recognizes Sarah as a dutiful wife: *"Sarah obeyed Abraham, and called him Sir"* (1599 Geneva Bible).

The Countess of Salisbury continued, "He who clips the edges of a coin or who counterfeits your stamped image on a coin shall die, my lord; will your sacred self commit high treason against the King of Heaven by stamping his image in forbidden metal, forgetting your allegiance and your oath?"

In this society, anyone who would cut the edges off a gold coin, thereby lessening its value, or who counterfeited a coin by using gold mixed with an alloy, would be sentenced to death. Such people were lessening the value of coins on which the King's image was stamped; this was a capital offense.

Genesis 1:27 states, *"Thus God created the man in his image: in the image of God created he him: he created them male and female"* (1599 Geneva Bible).

King Edward III was stamped with the image of God, but if he were to violate his marriage vows, he would be adulterating that image with sin. Such sin could be punished with damnation.

The Countess of Salisbury continued, "In violating marriage's sacred law, you break a greater honor than yourself. To be a King is of a younger ancestry than to be married; your progenitor, sole reigning Adam in the whole of creation, by God was honored for a married man, but not by him anointed for a King."

Marriage came into existence before Kingship did. Adam married Eve, but Adam was never anointed as a King.

She continued, "It is a criminal act to break your statutes, although they are not enacted with your highness' hand; how much more criminal it would be to infringe the holy act made by the mouth of God, sealed with His hand?

"I know my sovereign respects my husband, who is now doing loyal service in his sovereign's wars, and so my sovereign is only testing the wife of Salisbury to see whether or not she will listen to the tale of a seducer.

"Lest I be found guilty of that by my staying here, from that, and not from my liege, I turn away."

The Countess of Salisbury exited.

King Edward III said, "Which is it? Is her beauty made divine by her words, or are her words sweet chaplains to her beauty?

"Just as the wind beautifies a sail, and just as a sail graces the unseen wind, so do her words grace her beauty, and her beauty graces her words."

He knew that his wanting to sexually possess the Countess was wrong.

He added, "Oh, if only I were a honey-gathering bee that would bear the honeycomb of virtue from this flower, and not a poison-sucking malicious spider that would turn the juice I take to deadly venom.

"Religion is austere and beauty is gentle: too strict a guardian for so beautiful a ward.

"Oh, if only she were as is the air to me! Why so she is, for when I would embrace her, this I do" — he made an embracing movement in the air — "and I catch nothing but myself.

"I must enjoy her in bed, for I cannot beat my fond, foolish love away with reason and reproof."

The Earl of Warwick walked toward him.

"Here comes her father," King Edward III said. "I will persuade him to bear my battle flag in this battlefield of love."

The Earl of Warwick said, "How is it that my sovereign is so sad? May I with pardon know your highness' grief? If an effort by me, despite my age, can remove it, it shall not long burden your majesty."

"You are offering a kind and voluntary gift that I was eager to have begged of you," King Edward III said.

He then addressed the world: "But, oh, world, you great nurse of flattery, why do you tip men's tongues with golden words and weigh down their deeds with the weight of heavy lead, so that fair performance cannot follow promise?

"Oh, that a man might hold close the book of his heart, and choke the lavish tongue when it utters the breath of falsehood not engraved there!"

"Far be it from the honor of my age that I should own bright gold and render lead," the Earl of Warwick said. "Age is a critic, not a flatterer. I say again, that if I knew your grief and if that grief of yours by me may be lessened, my own harm would buy your highness' good. I would willingly harm myself if it would do you good."

King Edward III said, "These are the vulgar tenders of false men who never pay what their words have promised. You will not hesitate to swear what you have said, but when you know the circumstances of my grief, you will eat up again this rash disgorged vomit of your words and leave me helpless. You won't do what you have promised to do."

"By Heaven, I will not break my word," the Earl of Warwick said, "even if your majesty were to tell me to run upon your sword and die."

King Edward III said, "Let's say that my grief is in no way able to be cured except by the loss and bruising of your honor."

"If nothing but that loss may benefit you," the Earl of Warwick said, "I would regard that loss as my benefit, too."

King Edward III asked, "Do you think that you can unswear your oath and make it not an oath again?"

The Earl of Warwick replied, "I cannot, nor would I if I could."

King Edward III asked, "But if you do unswear your oath, what shall I say to you?"

The Earl of Warwick replied, "Say what may be said to any perjured villain who breaks the sacred warrant of an oath."

"What would you say to one who breaks an oath?" King Edward III asked.

The Earl of Warwick replied, "I would say to him that he has broken his faith with God and man, and from them both he stands excommunicated."

King Edward III asked, "Whose duty would it be to suggest to a man that he should break a lawful and religious vow?"

"That would be a duty for the devil, not for a man," the Earl of Warwick said.

King Edward III said, "That devil's duty you must do for me, or break your oath and cancel all the bonds of love and duty between yourself and me. And therefore, Earl of Warwick, if you are yourself the lord and master of your word and oath, go to your daughter — the Countess of Salisbury — and in my behalf command her, persuade her, and convince her by using any means to be my mistress and my secret love.

"I will not stand here and wait to hear you make a reply — your oath will either break her marriage oath or will let your sovereign die."

King Edward III exited.

"Oh, doting King," the Earl of Warwick said. "Oh, detestable duty! Well may I tempt myself to wrong myself when he has sworn me by the name of God to break a vow made by the name of God."

By "wrong myself," he meant "commit suicide."

The "vow made by the name of God" was his daughter's marriage vow.

He continued, "What if I swear by this right hand of mine to cut this right hand off? The better course of action would be to profane the idol than destroy it."

He meant that it would be better to treat the idol with contempt by not keeping the oath than to destroy the idol. One way to do that would be to disobey the idol. Here, the idol is his right hand, with which he had made an unvirtuous oath. Analogously, the idol is also an unvirtuous King. People in this culture believed that Kings ruled by divine right, but King Edward III was not behaving virtuously. Adultery could damn King Edward III to Hell.

The Earl of Warwick continued, "But I will do neither; I'll keep my oath, and to my daughter I'll make a recantation of all the virtue I have preached to her. Then I will recant the recantation.

"To be clear, I will tell her to do one thing, but make clear that she ought not to do that thing.

"I'll say she must forget her husband, the Earl of Salisbury, if she remembers — bears in mind — to embrace the King.

"I'll say an oath such as a marriage oath may easily be broken, but not so easily pardoned being broken.

"I'll say it is true charity to love, but not true love to be so charitable.

"I'll say the King's greatness may weather the shame, but not all of his Kingdom can buy out the sin.

"I'll say it is my duty to persuade her to break her marriage vow, but it is not the duty of her honesty and her loyalty to her husband to give consent to the King to sleep with her."

The Countess of Salisbury walked over to him.

Seeing her, the Earl of Warwick said, "See where she comes; no father ever had, against the benefit and well being of his child, an errand so bad."

The Countess of Salisbury said, "My lord and father, I have sought you. My mother and the peers urge you to stay in the presence of his majesty, and do your best to make his highness merry."

The Earl of Warwick thought, *How shall I begin this graceless errand? I must not call her child, for where's the father who will in such a courtship seduce his child? Then what about 'wife of Salisbury'? Shall I so begin? No, he's my friend, and where is found the friend who will do friendship such damage?*

He said out loud, "I call you neither my daughter, nor my dear friend's wife. I am not the Earl of Warwick as you think I am, but instead I am an attorney from the court of Hell, who thus have housed my spirit in his form in order to give you a message from the King."

Apparently, he meant that a demon from Hell had exchanged bodies with him for the purpose of delivering a Hellish message to her from the King.

He continued, "The mighty King of England dotes on you. He who has the power to take away your life also has the power to take away your honor, so then you should consent to pawn your honor rather than your life. Honor is often lost and gotten again, but life once gone has no recovery. The sun that withers hay also nourishes grass. The King who would defile you also will advance you. The ancient poets write that great Achilles' spear could heal the wound it made: The moral is that what mighty men misdo, they can amend."

The Greek warrior Achilles wounded Telephus with his spear, and the wound would not heal. Telephus eventually went to Achilles and promised to help the Greeks in their war against Troy if he would heal the wound. Rust from the head of the spear was scraped onto his wound, which healed.

The Earl of Warwick continued, "The lion dignifies its bloody jaws and shows mercy to its prey by being mild when the submissive vassal fearfully lies trembling at its feet.

"The King will in his glory hide your shame, and those who gaze on him to find you will lose their eyesight looking in the sun.

"How can one drop of poison harm the sea, whose huge vastness can digest the poison and make it lose its effect?

"The King's great name will temper your misdeeds, and give the bitter potion of reproach a sugared, sweet, and most delicious taste.

"Besides, it is no harm to do the thing that without shame could not be left undone. Not to obey a King is a shame, and so to obey a King is not a shame.

"In his majesty's behalf, I have thus dressed up sin in virtuous sentences, and I wait for your answer to the King's love suit."

His daughter the Countess replied, "Unnatural siege! Woe to unhappy me! I have escaped the danger of my foes and now I am ten times worse beset on by friends!

"Had the King no other means to stain my honest blood, but to corrupt the author of my blood — my father — to be his scandalous and vile solicitor?

"It is no marvel that the branches are then infected, when poison encompasses the root.

"It is no marvel that the poisoned infant dies, when the stern mother has poisoned her nipple.

"Why, then give sin a passport — official permission — to offend, and give youth the dangerous reign of liberty. Blot out the strict forbidding of the law, and cancel every canon law that prescribes a shame for shame, or penance for offence.

"No, let me die, if his too boisterous and savage will, will have it so, before I will consent to be an actor in his graceless lust."

The Earl of Warwick replied, "Why, just now you spoke as I would want you to speak. Pay close attention to how I unsay the words I just spoke:

"An honorable grave is more esteemed than the polluted private chamber of a King.

"The greater the man, the greater is the thing, whether it be good or bad, that he shall undertake.

"An insignificant speck of dust, flying in the sunshine, presents a greater substance than it is: It can be seen only in sunshine.

"The freshest summer's day soonest taints the loathed carrion that it seems to kiss.

"Deep are the blows made with a mighty axe.

"That sin that is committed in a holy place aggravates itself ten times. It is ten times more heinous because it is committed in a holy place.

"An evil deed done by authority — taking advantage by using one's power — is both sin and subornation, aka inducement, to sin.

"Deck an ape in rich clothing, and the beauty of the robe adds only the greater scorn to the beast.

"Daughter, I could urge a spacious field of many reasons to put between his glory and what would be your shame. Power and honor do not always go together:

"Poison shows worst in a golden cup.

"Dark night seems darker by the lightning flash.

"Lilies that fester smell far worse than weeds.

"And every glorious person who inclines to sin trebles his shame because he seeks the opposite of what a person with his advantages should seek.

"So I leave with my blessing in your bosom. This blessing will convert to a most heavy curse if you convert from honor's golden name to the black faction of bed-blotting shame."

His daughter the Countess said, "I'll follow you, and if my mind turns to such evil, may my body sink my soul in endless woe."

— 2.2 —

[Scene 4]

The Earl of Derby, who had just returned from France, and Lord Audley, who was accompanied by a military drummer, talked together.

The Earl of Derby said, "Thrice noble Lord Audley, you are well encountered here. It is good to see you. How is it with our sovereign King Edward III and his peers?"

Lord Audley replied, "It is fully a fortnight since I saw his highness. At that time he sent me forth to muster men, which I accordingly have done and have brought them hither before his majesty in fair readiness for combat. What news, my lord of Earl of Derby, do you have from the Emperor of Almagne?"

"As good as we desire," the Earl of Derby replied. "The Emperor has yielded friendly aid to his highness, and he makes our King lieutenant-general in all his lands and large dominions. So then *via* — let's go! — for the spacious bounds of France!"

Lord Audley asked, "Does his highness leap with gladness to hear this news?"

"I have not yet found the right time to tell him the news," the Earl of Derby said. "The King is unhappy in his private apartment, I don't know for what reason, but he gave the order that no one should interrupt him until after dinner. The Countess Salisbury and her father — the Earl of Warwick — as well as the Count of Artois and all the others, look downcast."

Lord Audley said, "Undoubtedly then something is wrong."

Trumpets sounded.

The Earl of Derby said, "The trumpets sound — the King is now out of his private apartment."

King Edward III entered the room.

"Here comes his highness," Lord Audley said.

The Earl of Derby said, "May all my sovereign's wishes come true."

King Edward III said, "Ah, I wish that you were a witch who could make it so."

"The Emperor of Almagne sends you greetings —" the Earl of Derby began.

King Edward III interrupted, "I wish the greetings came from the Countess of Salisbury."

The Earl of Derby finished, "— and has agreed to your highness' suit."

King Edward III replied, "You lie, she has not, but I wish that she had."

"I give all love and duty to my lord the King," Lord Audley said.

King Edward III replied, "Well, all but one is none."

In other words, the love and duty of everyone except the Countess of Salisbury is worth nothing.

He then asked Lord Audley, "What news do you bring?"

Lord Audley replied, "I have, my liege, levied those horse soldiers and foot soldiers as you ordered me to, and I have brought them hither."

King Edward III said, "Then let those foot soldiers trudge away from here immediately after those horse soldiers, according to our discharge, and be gone."

He added, "Earl of Derby, I'll look upon the Countess' mind soon."

He meant that he would look at her thoughts — her response to his proposition — that would be conveyed in a letter.

The Earl of Derby asked, "The Countess' mind, my liege?"

"I mean the Emperor of Almagne," King Edward III said.

He then ordered, "Leave me alone."

Lord Audley asked the Earl of Derby quietly, "What's in his mind? What is he thinking about?"

The Earl of Derby replied, "Let's leave him to his mood."

The Earl of Derby and Lord Audley exited, as did Lord Audley's military drummer.

King Edward III said, "Thus from the heart's abundance speaks the tongue: 'Countess' for 'Emperor,' and indeed why not? She is like an Emperor over me, and I to her am like a kneeling vassal who observes the pleasure or displeasure of her eye."

Lodowick entered the room.

King Edward III asked him, "What says the more than Cleopatra's match to Caesar now?"

The "more than Cleopatra's match" was the Countess of Salisbury.

Lodowick replied, "Still she says, my liege, that before night she will give your majesty her answer."

A drum sounded.

King Edward III said, "What drum is this that thunders forth this march to disturb the tender Cupid in my bosom? Poor sheepskin, how it brawls with the drummer who beats it."

Drums and parchment are made from sheepskin.

King Edward III continued, "Go wear out the thundering parchment bottom completely, and I will teach it to conduct sweet lines to the bosom of a Heavenly nymph, for I will use it as my writing paper, and so reduce the drum from a scolding drum to be the herald and dear counsel-bearer between a goddess and a mighty King."

He then ordered, "Go tell the drummer to learn to touch the lute or hang himself in the straps of his drum, for now we think it an uncivil thing to trouble Heaven with such harsh resounds. Go."

Lodowick exited.

King Edward III continued, "The quarrel that I have requires no arms but these arms of mine, and these shall meet my foe in a deep march of piercing groans. My eyes shall be my arrows, and my sighs shall serve me as the favor and advantage of the wind to whirl away my sweetest artillery.

"Ah, but alas, she wins the sun of me — the sun is in my eyes — because she herself is the sun, and therefore poets call the wanton warrior — Cupid — blind.

"But love has eyes as judgment to its steps, until too much loved glory dazzles them."

Lodowick returned, and King Edward III asked, "What is the source of that drumming?"

"My liege, the drummer who struck the lusty march accompanies Edward the Black Prince, your thrice valiant son," Lodowick answered.

Lodowick exited and Edward the Black Prince entered the room.

King Edward III thought, *I see the boy. Oh, how his mother's face, which is modeled in his face, corrects my strayed desire, and berates my heart and chides my thievish eye, which despite being rich enough in seeing her yet seeks elsewhere. The basest theft is that which cannot cloak itself in poverty. Some people justify theft on the basis that their poverty makes them steal, but my desire is not impoverished because I am married to such a good wife.*

He said to Edward the Black Prince, "Now, boy, what news do you bring?"

"I have assembled, my dear lord and father," Edward the Black Prince said, "the choicest buds of all our English blood for our affairs in France, and here we come to take orders from your majesty. We are ready to go fight in France when you order us to."

King Edward III thought, *Still I see delineated in him his mother's visage; his eyes are hers, eyes that looking attentively at me make me blush for faults and make me give evidence against myself.*

Lust is a fire, and men like lanterns show light — and show themselves alight, and wanton — lust within themselves, even through themselves.

Away, loose silks of wavering, inconstant vanity!

Shall I overthrow the extensive territory of fair Bretagne, and shall I not master this little mansion of myself?

Give me an armor of eternal steel! I go to conquer Kings! Shall I not then subdue myself?

Or shall I be my enemies' friend because I am unable to subdue myself? Shall I be my enemies' friend because I lack the self-control needed to conquer France?

It must not be.

He said to Edward the Black Prince, "Come, boy, forward, advance. Let's with our colors — our battle flags — sweeten the air of France."

Lodowick entered the room and said, "My liege, with a smiling face the Countess desires access to your majesty."

King Edward III thought, *Why, there my reformation goes; that very smile of hers has ransomed captive France and set the French King, the Dauphin, and the French peers at liberty.*

He said to Edward the Black Prince, "Go, leave me, Ned, and revel with your friends."

Edward the Black Prince exited.

King Edward III said to himself about his son Edward the Black Prince, "Your mother is but black, and you, because you are like her, make me remember how foul she is."

He then ordered Lodowick, "Go and fetch and escort the Countess here."

Lodowick exited.

King Edward III added to himself, "And let her chase away these winter clouds, for she gives beauty both to Heaven and Earth. It is a greater sin to hack and hew poor men in war than to embrace in an unlawful bed the register of all rarities since the time of leather-wearing Adam until this most recent hour."

Lodowick returned, escorting the Countess of Salisbury.

King Edward III ordered, "Go, Lodowick, put your hand into your purse and play, spend, give, riot, waste, do whatever you will, as long as you will go away from here for a while and leave me here."

Trusted servants often carried their master's moneybags, which this society called purses.

Lodowick exited.

King Edward III then said to the Countess of Salisbury, "Now, my soul's playfellow, have you come in your beauteous love to speak the more than Heavenly word of 'yes' to my proposition?"

The Countess of Salisbury said, "My father on his blessing has commanded —"

"— that you shall yield to me," King Edward III interrupted.

The Countess of Salisbury replied, "Yes, my dear liege, that I shall yield to you what is your due."

King Edward III said, "And that, my dearest love, can be no less than right for right, and love for love."

She replied, "— no less than wrong for wrong, and endless hate for hate. But since I see your majesty is so bent and inclined that my unwillingness, my husband's love, your high estate, and no regard for any other consideration can be my help, but that your mightiness will overrule and repress through awe and dread of your majesty these dear considerations, I will make myself be happy with what displeases me and I will force myself to do what I don't want to do, provided that you yourself remove those obstacles that stand between your highness' love and mine."

King Edward III said, "Name those obstacles, fair Countess, and I swear by Heaven that I will remove them."

The Countess of Salisbury said, "It is their lives that stand between our love that I would have suffocated, my sovereign."

"Whose lives, my lady?" King Edward III asked.

"My thrice loving liege," the Countess of Salisbury said, "the lives of your Queen and the Count of Salisbury, my wedded husband. These people while living have that title to our love that we cannot bestow except but by their death."

"What you are proposing is against the law," King Edward III objected.

"So is your desire," the Countess of Salisbury said. "If the law can prevent you from executing and carrying out the one, let it forbid you to attempt the other. I cannot think you love me as you say unless you make good on what you have sworn."

"Say no more," King Edward III said, "your husband and the Queen shall die. Fairer are you by far than Hero was, and beardless Leander is not as strong as I am. He swam an easy current for his love, but I will go through a Hellespont of blood to arrive at Sestos where my Hero lies."

In ancient Greek mythology, Leander was a man who loved the woman Hero, who was a priestess in a temple dedicated to the goddess Aphrodite at the town of Sestos. He used to swim across the Hellespont to see her, but he drowned one night. The modern name for the Hellespont is the Dardanelles.

"No, you'll do more," the Countess of Salisbury said, "you'll also make the river with the blood of the hearts of those two who keep our love asunder: my husband and your wife."

King Edward III said, "Your beauty makes them guilty and deserving of their death sentences, and gives evidence that they shall die, upon which verdict I, their judge, condemn them."

"Oh, perjured beauty, and more corrupted judge!" the Countess of Salisbury said. "When in the great Star Chamber — the Heavenly court — over our heads the universal sessions call to account this secret, underhand evil, we both shall tremble for it."

She was referring to the Last Judgment.

"What does my fair love say?" King Edward III asked. "Is she resolute?"

By "resolute," he meant "decided."

The Countess replied, "Resolute to be dissolved."

She meant that she was determined to die.

The King likely thought that she had decided to be dissolute.

She added, "And therefore I say this: Just keep your word, great King, and I am yours.

"Stand where you are standing, I'll go away a little from you, and see how I will yield myself to your hands."

She moved away from him and then made a reference to the two wedding knives that brides at that time wore in a sheath during their weddings:

"Here by my side hang my wedding knives: Take one, and with it kill your Queen. You can learn from me where you can find she lies; and with this other, I'll dispatch my love, my husband, who now lies fast asleep within my heart."

The King's Queen resided within his heart, just as the Countess' husband resided within her heart. She was proposing a double suicide.

She said, "When they are gone, then I'll consent to love you. Don't move, lascivious King, and don't try to stop me. My resolution is more nimbler by far than your attempted prevention can be if you try to rescue me and keep me from killing myself.

"If you move, I will strike my heart with my knife; therefore, stand still, and listen to the choice that I will put before you. Either swear to leave your most unholy love suit to me and swear to never henceforth solicit me, or else, by Heaven, this sharp-pointed knife shall stain your earth with that blood which you want to stain with dishonor: my poor chaste blood.

"Swear, Edward, swear, or I will strike my heart with my knife and die in front of you here."

She knelt.

King Edward III said, "Even by that Heavenly power I swear that gives me now the power to be ashamed of myself, I never mean to part my lips again in any words that tend to such a love suit.

"Arise, true English lady, whom our isle may better boast of than any Roman might boast of her whose ransacked treasury has tasked the vain endeavor of so many pens."

He was referring to Lucretia, an ancient Roman woman who committed suicide after being raped; this led to the throwing out of the Roman King and the establishment of the Roman Republic.

King Edward III continued, "Arise and let my sin be your honor's fame, which after ages shall enrich you with."

He raised her up from the floor and said, "I am awakened from this idle dream."

He then called, "Earl of Warwick, Edward the Black Prince, Earl of Derby, Count of Artois, and Lord Audley, brave warriors all, where are you all this while?"

All of the men he had named entered the room.

King Edward III said, "Earl of Warwick, I make you Warden of the North.

"You, Edward the Black Prince, and Lord Audley, go immediately to sea, hurry to Newhaven — some others are there waiting for me.

"I myself, the Count of Artois, and the Earl of Derby will travel through Flanders to greet our friends there and to ask for their aid.

"This night will scarcely suffice for me to reveal my folly's siege against a faithful lover, for before the sun shall gild the eastern sky we'll wake it with our martial harmony."

He planned to confess his sin this night.

CHAPTER 3
— 3.1 —
[Scene 5]

King John II of France, his two sons — Prince Charles Duke of Normandy and young Prince Philip — and the Duke of Lorraine met and talked together on the coast of France.

King John II of France said, "Here, until our navy of a thousand sails has devoured for breakfast our foe by sea, let us camp to wait for news of their happy success."

He then asked, "Duke of Lorraine, what readiness does King Edward III of England have? What have you heard about the military equipment he has for this exploit?"

The Duke of Lorraine answered, "To lay aside unnecessary soothing reassurance, and not to spend the time in unnecessary detail, it is reported for a certainty, my lord, that he's exceedingly strongly fortified. His subjects flock as willingly to war as if they were being led to a triumph."

Prince Charles Duke of Normandy said, "England is accustomed to harbor malcontents, bloodthirsty and seditious Catilines, spendthrifts, and such as yearn for nothing else but the changing and alteration of the state."

Catiline was an ancient Roman who wished to overthrow the Roman Republic.

Prince Charles Duke of Normandy continued, "Given this, is it possible that they are now so loyal in themselves?"

"All except the Scot, King David II, who solemnly protests, as heretofore I have informed his grace, never to sheathe his sword or make a truce with the English," the Duke of Lorraine said.

King John II of France said, "Ah, that's the anchorage of some better hope.

"But, on the other side, to think what friends King Edward III of England has retained in the Netherlands among those ever-imbibing epicures — those frothy Dutchmen puffed with double-strength beer, who drink and swill in every place they come — does not a little aggravate my ire.

"Besides, we hear that the Emperor of Almagne joins him and installs him in his own position of authority.

"But all the mightier that their number is, the greater glory reaps the victory. A victory against greater numbers achieves greater glory.

"Some friends have we besides our own domestic power: The stern, fierce Poles, the warlike Danes, the King of Bohemia, and the King of Sicily have all become confederates with us, and, as I think, are marching hither apace."

The Poles and the Danes were mercenaries.

Military drums sounded.

King John II of France said, "Be quiet. I hear the music of their drums, by which I guess that their approach is near."

The King of Bohemia and some Danish mercenaries arrived, and a Polish Captain with other soldiers arrived from a different direction.

The King of Bohemia said, "King John II of France, as league and our friendly close neighborly relations require when friends are in any way distressed, I come to aid you with my country's military forces."

The Polish Captain said, "And from great Moscovy, fearful to the Turk, and from lofty Poland, nurse of hardy men, I bring these mercenaries to fight for you; they willingly will fight for your cause."

Moscovy is Russia.

"Welcome, Bohemian King, and welcome, all," King John II of France said. "This your great kindness I will not forget; besides your plentiful rewards in crowns that from our treasury you shall receive, there comes a hare-brained nation decked in pride, the plunder of which will be a third gain. You will gain gratitude from me, crowns from me, and plunder from the defeated enemy.

"And now my hope is full, my joy complete.

"At sea we are as puissant as the force of Agamemnon in the haven of Troy."

Agamemnon led the Greeks against the Trojans in the Trojan War.

King John II of France continued, "By land, we compare in strength with Xerxes, whose soldiers were so numerous they drank up rivers in their thirst."

Xerxes twice tried to conquer the Greeks, but his military forces were defeated each time.

King John II of France continued, "Then Bayard-like, blind, overweening Ned, in his attempt to reach at our imperial diadem, will either be swallowed by the waves or hacked to pieces when he comes ashore."

Coming from King John II of France, "Ned" was an insulting nickname for King Edward III of England.

Bayard was the name of Charlemagne's horse, but the name later became proverbial for blind recklessness.

A mariner entered with news.

"Near to the coast I have descried, my lord, as I was busy in my watchful charge, the proud armada of King Edward III's ships, which, far off when I first saw them, seemed as if they were a grove of withered pines.

"But, as they drew near, their glorious bright aspect, their streaming flags wrought of colored silk, appeared like a meadow full of sundry flowers adorning the naked bosom of the earth. Majestic was the order of their course. Their ships were arranged like the horned circle of the moon, and on the top gallant of the flagship, and likewise all the handmaids of his train, the arms of England and the arms of France united are quartered equally by herald's art."

Because King Edward III claimed to be King of France as well as King of England, his flags bore the arms of both countries. Each flag was divided into four quarters. Two quarters displayed the British lion, and two displayed the French fleur-de-lis.

The mariner continued, "Thus quickly carried with a merry gale, they plow the ocean hitherward at full speed."

King John II of France asked, "Dare he already crop the fleur-de-lis?"

The fleur-de-lis appeared in the royal arms of France. King Edward III had cropped it — he was acting as if the arms of France were already his, even before fighting for them.

King John II of France continued, "I hope the honey being gathered thence, he with the spider will afterward approach and shall suck forth deadly venom from the leaves."

The honey was the fleur-de-lis, which was already cropped. What remained was the poison: the French armada and land soldiers. The spider possibly was Edward the Black Prince. "He" referred to King Edward III.

King John II of France then asked, "But where's our navy? How are they prepared to wing themselves with sails against this flight of ravens?"

He meant to insult the British, but ravens were ill omens of death.

The mariner answered, "They, having knowledge of the English armada brought to them by the scouts, broke from anchor immediately and, puffed with rage no otherwise than were their sails puffed with wind, set forth, as when the food-empty eagle flies to satisfy his hungry voracious gullet."

King John II of France gave the mariner some money and said, "There's something for your news. Return to your ship, and if you escape the bloody stroke of war and survive the conflict, come back here again, and let us hear the manner of the fight."

The mariner exited.

"In the meantime, my lords," King John II of France said, "it is best that we be dispersed to separate places lest they chance to land.

"First you, my lord, with your Bohemian troops shall pitch your battalions on the lower hand.

"My eldest son, Prince Charles Duke of Normandy, together with these Russian mercenaries, shall climb the higher ground another way.

"Here in the middle coast between you two, Prince Philip — my younger boy — and I will lodge.

"So, lords, go, and look after your command.

"You stand for France, an empire fair and large."

Everyone except King John II of France and Prince Philip, his youngest son, exited.

King John II of France said, "Now tell me, Philip, what is your opinion about the challenge to France that the English are making?"

Prince Philip answered, "I say, my lord, claim Edward III what he can, and bring he never so plain a pedigree, it is you who are in possession of the crown, and that's the surest point of all the law.

"But even if it were not, yet before he should prevail, I'll either make a conduit — a fountain — of my dearest blood or chase those straggling upstarts home again."

"Well said, young Philip," King John II of France said. "Call for bread and wine, so that we may cheer our stomachs with repast in order to look our foes more sternly in the face."

The noise of a sea battle sounded in the distance.

"Now is begun the heavy day at sea," King John II of France said. "Fight, Frenchmen, fight; be like the field of bears when they defend their younglings in their caves. Steer, angry Nemesis, the happy helm so that with the sulphur battles of your rage the English fleet may be dispersed and sunk."

The ancient Greek goddess Nemesis got vengeance against those who were arrogant toward the gods.

A cannon shot fired at sea.

Prince Philip said, "Oh, father, how this echoing cannon shot, like sweet harmony, digests the delicacies I am eating."

Sweet music was thought to be good for the digestion.

King John II of France said, "Now, boy, you hear what thundering terror it is to fight at close quarters for a Kingdom's sovereignty. The earth with giddy trembling when it shakes, or when the exhalations of the air break in extremity of lightning flash, frightens not more than Kings when they decide to show the rancor of their high-swollen hearts."

A signal for retreat sounded.

"Retreat is sounded," King John II of France said. "One side has the worse of the battle. Oh, if it should be the French, sweet Fortune turn, and in your turning change the adverse winds, so that with the advantage of a favoring sky our men may vanquish and the other men flee."

The mariner returned. He looked downcast.

"My heart misgives," King John II of France said.

He then said to the mariner, "Say, mirror of pale death, to whom belongs the honor of this day? Relate, I tell you, if your breath will serve, the sad discourse of this discomfiture."

"I will, my lord," the mariner said. "My gracious sovereign, France has been defeated, and boasting Edward III triumphs with success. These iron-hearted navies of France and of England, when last I was reporter to your grace, both full of angry temper, of hope and fear, hastening to meet each other face to face, at last conjoined, and by their flagship, our flagship encountered much cannon fire.

"By this ship, the other ships, which beheld these twain give promises of further destruction, like fiery dragons took their haughty flight, and, likewise meeting, from their smoky wombs sent many grim ambassadors of death.

"Then the day began to turn to gloomy night because of the smoke of cannon fire, and darkness did as well enclose the living as those who were but newly bereft of life.

"No leisure served for friends to bid farewell, and if it had, the hideous noise was such as each to the other seemed deaf and dumb. Red with blood was the sea, whose channel filled as fast with streaming gore that from the maimed fell, as did her gushing moisture break into the crannied fissures of the shot-through planks.

"Here flew a head dissevered from the trunk. There mangled arms and legs were tossed aloft, as when a whirlwind takes the summer dust and scatters it in the middle of the air.

"Then might you see the reeling vessels split in two, and tottering sink into the ruthless water until their lofty tops were seen no more.

"All tactics were tried both for defense and the hurt of offense, and now the effect of valor and of force, of resolution and of cowardice, were lively pictured: We saw how the one for fame and reputation, the other by compulsion laid about.

"Much did the *Nonpareil*, that brave ship without an equal. So did the *Black Snake* of Boulogne, than which a more splendid vessel never yet spread sail. But all in vain: The sun, as well as the wind and tide, all revolted against us and joined our foemen's side, so that we of necessity were forced to give way to them, and they landed on the beach.

"Thus my tale is done: We have inopportunely lost, and they have won."

King John II of France said, "Then remains there nothing to do but as quickly as we can to join our separate military forces all in one group and bid the enemy to battle before they range too far.

"Come, gentle Philip, let us from hence depart. This soldier's words have pierced your father's heart."

— 3.2 —

[Scene 6]

Two Frenchmen met a French woman, her two little children, and some other French citizens and began to talk together in a town. The two Frenchmen had traveled to the town, while the French woman, her children, and the other French citizens lived in the town but were preparing to flee.

"Well met, my masters," the first Frenchman said. "How is everything now? What's the news? And why are you laden thus with your belongings? Is it quarter day so that you are moving, and carrying your bag and baggage, too?"

"Quarter day" was the day that leases ran out, and so it was the day that families who did not renew the lease moved.

The first citizen said, "Quarter day, yes, and quartering day, I fear."

"Quartering day" was a grim pun. The bodies of executed criminals were sometimes quartered: cut into four parts.

The first citizen added, "Have you not heard the news that flies abroad?"

The first Frenchman asked, "What news?"

The second citizen said, "How the French navy is destroyed at sea, and the English army has arrived on French soil."

The first Frenchman asked, "So what, then?"

The first citizen said, "'So what, then?' said you? Why, isn't it time to flee, when enmity and destruction are so nigh?"

The first Frenchman said, "Calm down, man; they are far enough away from here, and they will be met, I assure you, to their cost before they break so far into the realm of France."

The first citizen said, "Yes, and so the grasshopper spends the time in mirthful jollity until winter comes, and then too late he would redeem and use better his time when frozen cold has nipped his neglectful head. He who no sooner will provide a cloak than when he sees it begin to rain, may very likely, for his negligence, be thoroughly soaked when he doesn't expect it.

"We who have responsibility and such a train of dependents as this must take timely actions to look after them and ourselves, lest when we would, we cannot be relieved. We must be prudent and take steps now to protect ourselves and our loved ones."

The second Frenchman said, "Probably you then fear ill results, and you think your country will be subjugated to the English."

The second citizen said, "We cannot tell; it is good to fear the worst."

The first Frenchman said, "Yet you should fight rather than, like unnatural sons, forsake your loving parents in distress."

The first citizen said, "Tush, they who have already taken up arms are many dread-inspiring millions in comparison to that small handful of our enemies. But it is true that a rightful quarrel must prevail. Edward III is the son of our late King's sister, whereas John Valois — King John II of France — is three degrees removed."

The Frenchwoman said, "Besides, there goes a prophecy abroad, published by one who was a friar once, whose oracles have many times proved to be true, and now, he says, the time will shortly come when a lion — the symbol of England — roused in the west shall carry away from here the fleur-de-lis of France. These I can tell you, and similar surmises strike many Frenchmen cold to the heart."

Another Frenchman arrived and said, "Flee, countrymen and citizens of France! Sweet flowering Peace, the root of happy life, has been quite abandoned and has been expelled from the French land. Instead of Peace, War — which inevitably leads to looting — sits like evil-omened ravens on your houses' tops. Slaughter and Evil walk within your streets and unrestrained make havoc as they pass.

"The form of such horrifying things just now I myself beheld, upon this fair mountain from whence I came" — he pointed to the mountain — "for so far off as I directed my eyes, I perceived five cities all on fire, cornfields and vineyards burning like an oven; and as the smoke rising in the wind turned aside and cleared a little, I likewise discerned the poor inhabitants, having escaped the flame, falling numberless upon the soldiers' pikes.

"Three ways these dreadful ministers of wrath tread the measures of their tragic march. Upon the right comes the conquering King Edward III. Upon the left comes his hot unbridled son, Edward the Black Prince. And in the midst is their nation's glittering armed multitude of their best soldiers. All three of these parts, though distant, yet conspire as one to leave behind desolation wherever they have come.

"Flee, therefore, citizens. If you are wise, seek some habitation further off. Here if you stay, your wives will be abused, your treasure shared before your weeping eyes. Shelter yourselves, for now the storm does rise."

The treasure consisted of the citizens' wives.

The Frenchman continued, "Leave! Leave! I think I hear their drums!

"Ah, wretched France, I greatly fear you will fall. Your glory shakes like a tottering wall."

— 3.3 —

[Scene 7]

King Edward III and the Earl of Derby stood together. Also present were some English soldiers and the French prisoner Gobin de Grace.

King Edward III asked, "Where's the Frenchman by whose cunning guide we found the ford of this Somme River and received instructions about how to pass the estuary?"

Gobin de Grace said, "Here I am, my good lord."

"What are you called?" King Edward III said. "Tell me your name."

"My name is Gobin de Grace, if it please your excellence."

"Then, Gobin, for the service you have done," King Edward III said, "we here set you at large and give you liberty, and for recompense in addition to this freedom, you shall receive five hundred marks in gold."

Gobin de Grace exited.

Using the royal plural, King Edward III said, "Without his help, I don't know how we would have met our son, whom now in heart I wish I might behold."

The Count of Artois arrived and said, "Good news, my lord. The Prince is close at hand, and with him comes Lord Audley and the rest, whom since our landing we have not been able to meet."

Edward the Black Prince, Lord Audley, and some soldiers arrived.

"Welcome, fair Prince," King Edward III said. "How have you sped, my son, since your arrival on the coast of France?"

Edward the Black Prince said, "We have sped successfully, and I thank the gracious Heavens. Some of their strongest cities we have won, including Barfleur, Lô, Crotoy, and Carentan, and others we have laid waste to, leaving at our heels a wide apparent wasteland and beaten path for solitariness to progress in. Yet those who would submit we kindly pardoned, but those who in scorn refused our proffered peace have endured the penalty of sharp revenge."

"Ah, France, why should you be this obstinate against the kind embracement of your friends?" King Edward III said. "How gently had we thought to touch your breast and set our foot upon your tender earth, but in perverse, obstinate, and disdainful pride you, like a skittish and untamed colt, startle and then strike us with your heels.

"But tell me, Ned, in all your warlike course, have you seen the usurping King of France?"

"Yes, my good lord, and not two hours ago," Edward the Black Prince said. "I saw him with his multitudes. Fully a hundred thousand French fighting men were upon both sides of the river's bank.

"I feared that he would cut down our smaller army, but fortunately, perceiving your approach, he and his soldiers have withdrawn to the plains of Crécy, where, as it appears by his good array of soldiers, he intends to bid us to fight soon."

King Edward III said, "He shall be welcome — that's the thing we crave."

King John II of France, Prince Charles Duke of Normandy, the Duke of Lorraine, the King of Bohemia, young Prince Philip, and some French soldiers arrived.

King John II of France said, "Edward, know that John, the true King of France, astonished that you should encroach upon his land and in your tyrannous proceeding slay his faithful subjects and overthrow his towns, spits in your face, and upbraids you with your arrogant invasion for these reasons:

"First, I condemn you and say that you are a vagrant, a thievish pirate, and an unworthy fellow — you are one who has either no abiding place, or else, inhabiting some barren soil where neither herbs nor fruitful grains can be had, you live entirely by pilfering.

"Next, insofar as you have infringed your faith, broken your league and solemn covenant made with me, I regard you as a false pernicious wretch.

"And last of all, although I scorn to come into contact with one so much inferior to myself, yet because your thirst is all for gold, your labor rather to be feared than loved, to satisfy your lust in either part here have I come, and with me I have brought an exceedingly great store of treasure, pearls, and coin."

The words "your labor rather to be feared than loved" were ambiguous. They could mean 1) you labor to make yourself feared rather than loved, and/ or 2) your labors (in making war) are rather to be feared than loved.

In *The Prince* Niccolo Machiavelli wrote that "it is far safer to be feared than loved" (Ninian Hill Thomson translation).

King John II continued, "Cease therefore now to persecute the weak, and armed entering conflict with the armed, let it be seen among other petty thefts how you can win this pillage manfully. Let your army fight my army, and see if you can win this treasure by force of arms."

King Edward III said, "If gall or wormwood has a pleasant taste, then your salutation to me is honey-sweet. But since gall and wormwood do not have a pleasant taste, so your salutation to me is most satirical and ironic.

"Yet learn how I regard your worthless taunts: If you have uttered them to dishonor my fame or dim the reputation of my birth, know that your wolfish barking cannot hurt me.

"If you have uttered your worthless taunts slyly to insinuate your false opinions with the world, and with a strumpet's artificial lines of makeup to paint over and prettify your vicious and deformed cause, be well assured that the counterfeit will fade, and in the end your foul defects will be revealed and seen.

"But if you did it to provoke me on, as one who should say I were only timorous or, should I say, coldly negligent, did need a spur, then think to yourself how slack I was at sea.

"Now since my landing I have won no towns, entered no further than upon the coast, and there I have ever since securely slept.

"But if I have been employed otherwise than in sacking cities, guess, Valois, whether I intend to skirmish not for pillage, but for the crown that you wear and that I vow to have. The right answer involves one of us falling into his grave."

King Edward III was calling John "Valois" because before he had become King John II of France, he had been "John of Valois."

Edward the Black Prince said, "Don't look for cross, angry invectives at our hands or railing execrations of contempt. Let creeping serpents hidden in hollow banks sting with their tongues; we have remorseless swords, and they shall plead for us and our affairs.

"Yet, thus much briefly, by my father's leave, let me say that as all the immodest poison of your throat is scandalous and most notorious lies, and our proposed claim to the crown of France is truly just, so end the battle when we meet today — the one with the just claim to the French crown shall prosper and prevail, and the other, luckless and cursed, shall receive eternal shame."

King Edward III said, "Who has the rightful title to the French crown needs no further questioning, and I know that John's conscience witnesses that it is my right.

"Therefore, Valois, say if you will resign as King of France before the sickle's thrust into the corn, and before enkindled fury turns to flame?"

King John II of France said, "Edward, I know what 'right' you have in France, and before I basely will resign my crown, this level, open field shall be a pool of blood and all in our field of view shall be like a slaughterhouse."

Edward the Black Prince said, "Yes, that proves, tyrant, what you are: You are no father, King, or shepherd of your realm; instead, you are one who tears the realm's entrails with your hands, and like a thirsty tiger sucks her blood."

Lord Audley asked, "You peers of France, why do you follow him — a man who is so wastefully prodigal in spending your lives?"

Prince Charles Duke of Normandy asked Lord Audley, who was an older man, "Whom should they follow, aged impotent, but that man who is their true-born sovereign?"

King Edward III said, "Do you upbraid Lord Audley because time has engraved deep wrinkles of age in his face? Know that these grave scholars of experience, like stiff-grown oaks, will stand immovable when a whirlwind quickly turns up younger trees."

The Earl of Derby said to King John II, "Were any of your father's house ever King except yourself before this present time? Edward's great lineage, by the mother's side, has for five hundred years reigned and held the scepter up. Judge then, conspirators, by this descent who is the true-born sovereign."

He pointed to John II and then to Edward III as he asked, "This man or that man?"

Prince Philip said to King John II, "Father, arrange your battle formation and chatter no more. These Englishmen willingly would spend the time in exchanging words so that, with night approaching, they might escape without having fought."

King John II of France said to the Frenchmen, "Lords and my loving subjects, now's the time that your resolved military forces must undergo the test. Therefore, my friends, consider this in brief:

"He whom you fight for is your natural King. He against whom you fight is a foreigner. He whom you fight for rules in clemency and governs you with reins of a mild and kind and gentle bit. He against whom you fight, if he should prevail will immediately enthrone himself in tyranny, make slaves of you, and with a heavy hand curtail and curb your sweetest liberty.

"So then to protect your country and your King, let but the haughty courage of your hearts answer the number of your able hands, and we shall quickly chase after these fugitives.

"For what's this Edward but a belly-god, a man who makes a god of his sexual appetite, a man of tender and lascivious wantonness, who just the other day was almost dead for love?

"And what, I ask you, is his goodly guard? They are such soldiers that if you deprive them of their joints of beef and take away their downy featherbeds, then immediately they are as rusty and stiff from over-rest as if they were so many over-ridden jades.

"So then, Frenchmen, scorn that such should be your lords, and instead bind them in captive bands."

All the Frenchmen shouted, "*Vive le roi!* God save King John II of France!"

King John II of France said, "Now on this plain of Crécy spread yourselves, and Edward, when you dare, begin the fight."

King John II of France, the King of Bohemia, and all the Frenchmen exited.

King Edward III said as they exited, "We soon will meet you, John of France, in battle."

He then said, "And, English lords, let us resolve on the day, either to clear us of that scandalous crime, or be entombed in our innocence."

The scandalous crime he was accused of was trying to usurp the crown of France.

King Edward III said to Edward the Black Prince, "And, Ned, because this battle is the first ever that you will fight in a pitched field, as it is the ancient custom of martialists and soldiers to dub you with the emblems of chivalry, we will give you arms in solemn manner."

He then ordered, "Come therefore, heralds. Orderly bring forth strong military equipment for Edward the Black Prince, my son."

Four heralds brought in a coat of armor, a helmet, a lance, and a shield. King Edward III took the coat of armor, the Earl of Derby took the helmet, Lord Audley took the lance, and the Count of Artois took the shield.

King Edward III said, "Edward Plantagenet, in the name of God, as with this armor I enfold your breast, may your noble unrelenting heart be walled in with flint of matchless fortitude so that base affections never enter there. Fight and be valiant; conquer wherever you go.

"Now follow, lords, and do him honor, too."

The Earl of Derby said, "Edward Plantagenet, Prince of Wales, as I set this helmet on your head, wherewith the chamber of your brain is fenced, so may your temples by Bellona's hand be always adorned with the laurel wreath of victory. Fight and be valiant; conquer wherever you go."

Bellona is the Roman goddess of war.

Lord Audley said, "Edward Plantagenet, Prince of Wales, receive this lance in your manly hand. Use it in the fashion of a pen made of bronze to draw forth bloody stratagems in France and print your valiant deeds in honor's book. Fight and be valiant; conquer wherever you go."

The Count of Artois said, "Edward Plantagenet, Prince of Wales, grasp and take this shield, wear it on your arm and may the view of this shield, like Perseus' shield, astonish and transform your gazing foes to senseless images of gaunt death. Fight and be valiant; conquer wherever you go."

King Edward III said, "Now nothing is lacking except knighthood, which we defer and leave until you have won it in the battlefield."

"My gracious father and you leading peers," Edward the Black Prince said, "this honor you have done me animates and cheers my young and green, still scarcely appearing, strength with comforting signs of good things to come. No otherwise did old Jacob's words when he breathed his blessings on his sons. When I profane these hallowed gifts of yours or don't use them for the glory of my God or to provide patronage for the fatherless and poor, or for the benefit of England's peace, then let my joints be numb, both my arms grow feeble, and my heart wither so that, like a sapless tree, I may remain the epitome of infamy."

King Edward III said, "This is how our ranks of steel-brandishing soldiers shall be arranged.

"The leading of the vanguard, the foremost division, Ned, is yours. To dignify your lusty spirit all the more, we temper it with Lord Audley's gravity, so that, with courage and experience joined in one, your management of your troops may be second to none.

"As for the main fighting forces, I will guide them myself, and the Earl of Derby with troops in the rear will march behind the other forces.

"With the soldiers orderly arranged and set in readiness for combat, let us mount our horses and may God grant us the victory."

<h1 style="text-align:center">— 3.4 —</h1>

<h1 style="text-align:center">[Scene 8]</h1>

The Battle of Crécy was in progress. Edward the Black Prince pursued many fleeing Frenchmen.

King John II of France and the Duke of Lorraine talked together.

King John II of France said, "Oh, Duke of Lorraine, tell me, why are our men fleeing? Our soldiers number far greater than our foes."

The Duke of Lorraine answered, "The garrison of the Genoese, my lord, who came from Paris, weary with their long march, grudging to be immediately employed in battle, no sooner in the forefront took their place but they immediately retreated and so dismayed the rest of the soldiers that they likewise betook themselves to flight. In this flight, out of the soldiers' haste to make a safe escape, a thousandfold more are being pressed to death in the clustering throng than are being killed by the enemy."

"Oh, luckless fortune!" King John II of France said. "Let us yet try to see if we can persuade some of our soldiers to stay and fight."

In another part of the battlefield, King Edward III and Lord Audley talked together.

King Edward III said, "Lord Audley, while our son is in the chase after the fleeing French soldiers, withdraw our troops to this little hill, and here for a brief time let us rest ourselves."

"I will, my lord," Lord Audley said.

He exited.

A retreat sounded.

King Edward III said, "Justly ordaining Heaven, whose secret providence is inscrutable to our gross judgment, how we are bound to praise your wondrous works that have this day given way to the right, and made the wicked stumble at themselves."

Psalm 27:2 states, "*When the wicked, even mine enemies and my foes came upon me to eat up my flesh, they stumbled and fell*" (1599 Geneva Bible).

The Count of Artois arrived and said, "Rescue, King Edward III, rescue your son!"

King Edward III asked, "Rescue my son, Count of Artois? Is he taken prisoner? Or has he by violence fallen and is dead beside his horse and so I need to rescue his corpse?"

"Neither, my lord," the Count of Artois answered, "but he is narrowly beset by Frenchmen whom he pursued but who turned around and attacked him, and it is impossible that he will escape unless your highness will immediately descend from the hill and rescue him."

"Tut, let him fight," King Edward III said. "We gave him arms today, and he is laboring to earn a knighthood, man."

The Earl of Derby arrived and said, "The Prince, my lord, the Prince! Oh, help him! He's closely surrounded with a world of odds against him!"

Using the royal plural, King Edward III said, "Then he will win a world of honor, too, if he can free himself from thence by the use of his valor. If not, what does it matter? We have more sons than one to comfort us in our declining age."

Lord Audley arrived and said, "Renowned Edward, give me permission, I ask you, to lead my soldiers where I may relieve your grace's son, who is in danger of being slain. The snares of the French soldiers, like ants on an ant-hill, muster about him while he, lion-like, entangled in the net of their assaults, franticly rends and bites the woven net, but all in vain — he cannot free himself."

"Lord Audley, be calm," King Edward III said. "I will not have a man, on pain of death, sent forth to help him. This is the day, ordained by destiny, on which if he breaks out without help from others, he will season his courage with impressive memories — impressive memories that he will take pleasure in even if he lives as long as Nestor, the Greeks' old warrior-advisor in the Trojan War."

The Earl of Derby said, "Ah, but he shall not live to see those aged days."

King Edward III replied, "Why, then his epitaph — his reputation after death — will be lasting praise."

Lord Audley said, "Yet, my good lord, it is too much willfulness to let his blood be spilled when it may be saved."

King Edward III ordered, "Exclaim no more, for none of you can tell whether a borrowed aid — the help of others — will serve or not. Perhaps he is already slain or captured.

"If you make a falcon tremble and be afraid when she's in her flight, forever after she'll be untrainable. Let Edward be delivered from danger by our hands, and then whenever he's in danger he'll expect to be rescued, but if he frees himself from danger, he will have vanquished, cheerfully, death and fear, and forever after dread their force no more than if they were but babes or captive slaves."

Apparently, he meant that it was best for Edward the Black Prince to fight against the odds. He would have two outcomes: to win or to be defeated. He would win by fighting and not by trembling; fighting against the odds can concentrate the mind wonderfully so that fear is conquered. But if he were to be rescued, he would learn the danger he was in, and he would be afraid the next time he was in that situation.

"Oh, cruel father!" Lord Audley said. "Farewell, Prince Edward, then."

"Farewell, sweet Prince, the hope of chivalry," the Earl of Derby said.

"Oh, I wish that my life might ransom him from death," the Count of Artois said.

A retreat sounded.

King Edward III said, "Be quiet. I think I hear the dismal charge of trumpets' loud retreat. All are not slain, I hope, who went with him. Some will return with tidings, good or bad."

Edward the Black Prince arrived, in triumph, bearing in his hand his shivered lance. Ahead of him, the body of the King of Bohemia, wrapped in one of his battle flags and some other cloths, was carried. The Englishmen ran and embraced him.

Lord Audley said, "Oh, joyful sight — victorious Edward lives!"

"Welcome, brave Prince," the Earl of Derby said.

"Welcome, Plantagenet," King Edward III said.

Edward the Black Prince knelt and kissed his father's hand.

He then said, "First, Lords, I having done my duty as was fitting, greet you all again with hearty thanks. And now, behold, after my winter's toil, my painful voyage on the boisterous, tempestuous sea of war's devouring gulfs and hard-as-steel rocks, I bring my freight into the wished-for port, my summer's hope, my travel's sweet reward.

"And here with humble duty I present this sacrifice, this first fruit of my sword, cropped and cut down even at the gate of death, the King of Bohemia, father, whom I slew, whose thousands had entrenched me round about, and lay blows with their ponderous spears as thickly upon my battered helmet as on an anvil.

"Yet courage as enduring as marble always propped me up, and when my weary arms with frequent blows, like the continually laboring woodman's ax that is used to fell a load of oaks, began to falter, immediately I would remember the gifts you gave to me and I would remember my zealous vow, and then new courage made me fresh again, with the result that, in contempt, I carved my passage forth to safety and put the multitude of the enemy to speedy flight."

A soldier arrived, carrying Edward the Black Prince's sword.

Edward the Black Prince continued, "Lo, thus has Edward's hand fulfilled your request and has done, I hope, the duty of a knight."

King Edward III said, "Yes, you have well deserved a knighthood, Ned."

Edward the Black Prince knelt, and King Edward III took the Black Prince's sword from the soldier and then said, "And therefore with your sword, still smoking with the warm blood of those who fought to be your bane, I dub you knight."

King Edward III dubbed the Black Prince on the shoulders with the sword and said, "Arise, Prince Edward, trusty knight at arms. This day you have stunned me with joy and proven yourself to be a fit heir to a King."

Edward the Black Prince said, "Here is a list, my gracious lord, of those of our foes who in this conflict were slain."

He read the list out loud:

"*Eleven princes of esteem, fourscore barons,*

"*A hundred and twenty knights,*

"*And thirty thousand common soldiers;*

"*And of our men, a thousand.*"

"Our God be praised!" King Edward III said. "Now, John II of France, I hope that you know King Edward III is not a libertine or a love-sick sissy, and I hope that you know that his soldiers are not broken-down animals. But by which way has the fear-filled King escaped?"

"Towards Poitiers, noble father — and his sons went there, too," Edward the Black Prince said.

King Edward III ordered, "Ned, you and Lord Audley shall pursue them still, I and the Earl of Derby will go to Calais immediately, and there we will surround that haven town with a siege.

"Now the war lies on an upshot, so therefore strike, and intently follow them while the game's afoot."

An upshot is the final shot in an archery contest. In a close competition, the final shot determines the winner.

Seeing a picture on a cloth that was covering the King of Bohemia's corpse, King Edward III asked, "What picture's this?"

Edward the Black Prince answered, "A pelican, my lord, wounding her bosom with her crooked beak, so that her nest of young ones might be fed with the drops of blood that issue from her heart. The motto is *Sic et vos:* 'And so should you.'"

This may be seen as a criticism of King Edward III's decision to allow his son to fight against the odds. Or it may be seen as a criticism of any enemy who would not allow their young ones to fight against the odds.

CHAPTER 4
— 4.1 —
[Scene 9]

Lord Mountfort, who was holding a coronet in his hand, talked with the Earl of Salisbury.

Lord Mountfort said, "My lord of Salisbury, since by your aid my enemy, Sir Charles of Blois, has been slain and I am again quietly possessed of Bretagne's dukedom, know that I resolve, for this kind assistance of your King and you, to swear allegiance to his majesty, in token whereof receive this coronet. Bear it to King Edward III, and also bear my oath to never be anything but Edward III's faithful friend."

The Earl of Salisbury took the coronet from Lord Mountfort and said, "I do take it, Lord Mountfort, and like this I hope before long the whole dominions of the realm of France will be surrendered to King Edward III's conquering hand."

Lord Mountfort exited.

Alone, the Earl of Salisbury said to himself, "Now, if I only knew how to pass through France safely, I would gladly meet his grace King Edward III at Calais, where I am reliably informed by letters that he intends to have his army moved."

He thought a moment, came up with a plan, and said, "It shall be so; this plan will serve."

He then called, "Ho, who's within? Bring Villiers to me."

Villiers, a French lord, walked into the room.

The Earl of Salisbury said, "Villiers, you know you are my prisoner, and that I might, if I would, require from you one hundred thousand francs for ransom, or else I could retain and keep you captive always.

"But it is possible that for a smaller charge you may be released from paying that huge sum and if you are willing, you yourself will be released.

"And this is how that can happen: Just procure for me a passport from Prince Charles Duke of Normandy, so that I, without constraint, may have recourse to Calais through all the regions where he has power."

A passport is a document allowing the bearer to travel safely and without fear of arrest through a particular region.

He continued, "This passport you may easily obtain, I think, because I have often heard you say that Prince Charles Duke of Normandy and you were students once together. If you will do this, then you shall be set at liberty. What do you say? Will you undertake to do it?"

Villiers said, "I will, my lord, but I must speak with him."

"Why, so you shall," the Earl of Salisbury said. "Take a horse and ride posthaste away from here. Only, before you go, swear by your faith that if you cannot accomplish what I want that you will return and be my prisoner again. Your oath shall be sufficient warrant for me."

Villiers said, "To that condition I agree, my lord, and I will honestly keep my oath."

He exited.

"Farewell, Villiers," the Earl of Salisbury said. "For just this once I mean to try a French man's faith."

— 4.2 —

[Scene 10]

King Edward III and the Earl of Derby talked together. Some English soldiers were present. They were in front of the walls of Calais.

King Edward III said, "Since they refuse our proffered league, my lord, and will not open their gates and let us in, we will entrench ourselves on every side so that neither food nor any supply of men may come to help and succor this accursed town. Famine shall do combat where our swords are stopped."

Six poor Frenchmen came out of the city of Calais.

The Earl of Derby said, "The promised aid that made them stand aloof has now retired and gone another way: John II will not relieve them. The men of Calais will repent of their stubborn will."

Seeing the six poor Frenchmen, he asked, "But who are these poor ragged slaves, my lord?"

King Edward III ordered, "Ask who they are; it seems they come from Calais."

The Earl of Derby said to the six poor Frenchmen, "You wretched pictures of despair and woe, who are you — living men or gliding ghosts who have crept from your graves to walk upon the earth?"

The first poor Frenchman answered, "No ghosts, my lord, but men who breathe a life far worse than is the quiet sleep of death. We are distressed poor inhabitants who long have been diseased, sick, and lame, and now because we are not fit to serve, the Captain of the town of Calais has thrust us out so that some expense for food may be saved."

King Edward III said sarcastically, "A charitable deed no doubt, and worthy of praise!"

He then asked, "But how do you think then you will survive? We are your enemies in any case. We can do no less but put you to the sword and kill you because when we offered a truce, it was refused."

The first poor Frenchman said, "If your grace can do no otherwise than kill us, know that to us death is as welcome as life."

63

King Edward III said, "You are poor defenseless men, much wronged and more distressed."

He ordered, "Go, Earl of Derby, go, and see that they are given help. Command that food be given to them, and give to everyone five crowns apiece."

The Earl of Derby and the six poor Frenchmen exited.

King Edward III said to himself, "The lion scorns to touch the yielding prey, and Edward's sword must plunge itself in the flesh of such men as willful stubbornness has made perverse and intransigent."

Seeing Lord Percy arrive, King Edward III said, "Lord Percy, welcome. What's the news in England?"

Lord Percy answered, "The Queen, my lord, comes here to Calais to your grace, and from her highness and the lord vicegerent I bring these happy tidings of success: King David II of Scotland, who was recently up in arms, thinking perhaps that he would very quickly prevail since your highness is absent from the realm, by the fruitful service of your peers — and the painstaking travail of the Queen herself who, despite being big with child, was every day in arms — has been vanquished, subdued, and taken prisoner."

"Thanks, Percy, for your news with all my heart," King Edward III said. "What manner of man was he who captured him and made him prisoner on the battlefield?"

"A squire, my lord," Lord Percy answered. "John Copland is his name, who since entreated by her majesty, denies to make surrender of his prize to any but to your grace alone, at which the Queen is grievously displeased."

"Well, then we'll have a royal messenger dispatched to summon Copland hither out of hand," King Edward III said, "and with him he shall bring his royal prisoner."

Lord Percy said, "The Queen herself, my lord, is by this time sailing at sea, and as soon as the wind will allow her she intends to land at Calais and to visit you."

"She shall be welcome," King Edward III said, "and to await her coming I'll pitch my tent close to the sandy shore."

A Captain of Calais arrived and said, "The burgesses of Calais, mighty King, have by a counsel willingly decreed to yield the town and castle to your hands, upon the condition that it will please your grace to grant them benefit of life and goods."

"They will so?" King Edward III said sarcastically. "Then perhaps they may command, dispose, elect, and govern as they wish."

He then said seriously, "No, sirrah, tell them that since they refused our Princely clemency when it was at first proclaimed, they shall not have it now although they want it. I will accept nothing but fire and sword, unless, within these next two days, six of the men who are the wealthiest merchants in the town come to me entirely naked except for their linen shirts. Each rich merchant will wear a halter hung about his neck and will prostrate yield himself to me upon his knees to be afflicted, hanged, or whatever I please. And so you may inform their masterships."

Everyone except the Captain of Calais exited.

Alone, he said to himself, "Why, this is what it means to trust a broken staff. Had we not been persuaded that John II our King would with his army relieve the town, we would not have stood upon defiance so. But no man can recall time that has passed, and it is better that some go to destruction rather than that all go."

[Scene 11]

Prince Charles Duke of Normandy and Villiers spoke together.

"I marvel, Villiers," Prince Charles Duke of Normandy said, "that you should beg me for a favor for someone who is our deadly enemy."

Villiers replied, "It is not for his sake, my gracious lord, that I have so much become an earnest advocate, as that by my doing this my ransom will be quit."

"Your ransom, man?" Prince Charles Duke of Normandy said. "Why do you need to talk about that? Aren't you free? And aren't all occasions that happen to give us an advantage over our foes to be accepted, and stood upon?"

"No, my good lord, unless the occasions are just," Villiers said, "for profit must with honor be combined, or else our actions are simply scandalous. But letting pass these intricate objections, will it please your highness to sign the passport or not?"

"Villiers, I will not and I cannot do it," Prince Charles Duke of Normandy said. "The Earl of Salisbury shall not have his will so much to claim a passport from me at his own convenience."

"Why then I know the outcome, my lord," Villiers said. "I must return to the prison from which I came."

"Return!" Prince Charles Duke of Normandy said. "I hope you will not. What bird that has escaped the fowler's snare will not beware lest she's ensnared again? Or what man is so senseless and overconfident that, having with great difficulty passed a dangerous gulf, he will put himself in peril there again?"

"Ah, but it is my oath, my gracious lord," Villiers said, "which I in conscience may not violate. If not for my oath, a Kingdom should not draw me away from here."

"Your oath!" Prince Charles Duke of Normandy said. "Why, your oath binds you to stay here. Haven't you sworn obedience to your Prince?"

"Yes, in all things that uprightly and honorably he commands," Villiers said. "But either to persuade or threaten me to make me not perform the covenant of my word is lawless and dishonorable, and I need not obey."

Prince Charles Duke of Normandy said, "Why, is it lawful for a man to kill, and not to break a promise with, his foe?"

Villiers replied, "To kill, my lord, when war is once proclaimed, so that our quarrel is for wrongs received, no doubt is lawfully permitted us. But in an oath we must be well advised to what we swear, and, when we once have sworn, not to infringe it although we die therefore. Therefore, my lord, as willingly I return to prison as if I were to fly to Paradise."

He started to leave.

"Stay, my Villiers," Prince Charles Duke of Normandy said. "Your honorable mind deserves to be eternally admired. Your suit to me shall be no longer thus deferred — give me the paper; I'll sign my name to it, and while until now I loved you as Villiers, hereafter I'll embrace you as if you were myself. Stay, and be always in favor with your lord."

"I humbly thank your grace," Villiers said. "I must dispatch and send this passport first to the Earl of Salisbury, and then I will attend upon your highness' pleasure."

"Do so, Villiers," Prince Charles Duke of Normandy said, and then, referring to himself, added, "and may Charles' soldiers, when he has need, be like you, Villiers, whatever happens to him."

Villiers exited.

King John II of France entered the room and said, "Come, Charles, and arm yourself: Edward the Black Prince is trapped. The Prince of Wales has fallen into our hands, and we have surrounded him — he cannot escape."

"But will your highness fight today?" Prince Charles Duke of Normandy asked.

"What else, my son?" King John II of France replied. "He's scarcely eight thousand soldiers strong, and we have threescore thousand soldiers at the least."

Prince Charles Duke of Normandy said, "I have a prophecy, my gracious lord, wherein is written what outcome is likely to happen to us in this outrageous war. It was delivered me on Crécy's battlefield by a man who is an aged hermit there."

He read the prophecy out loud:

"When feathered fowl shall make your army tremble,

"And flintstones rise and break the battle array,

"Then think on him who does not now dissemble,

"For that shall be the hapless dreadful day;
"Yet in the end your foot you shall advance,
"As far in England as your foe in France."

King John II of France said, "According to this prophecy, it seems we shall be fortunate. For as it is impossible that stones should ever rise and break the battle array, or airy fowl make men in arms quake, so is it likely we shall not be subdued.

"Or let's say these things might be true and might happen, yet in the end, since the hermit promises we shall drive the English hence and ravage their country as they have done ours, with that revenge our loss will seem the less.

"But all such prophecies are frivolous fancies, trifles, and dreams. Once we are sure we have ensnared the son, we will afterward catch the father however we can."

— 4.4 —

[Scene 12]

Edward the Black Prince and Lord Audley talked together. Some English soldiers were present.

Edward the Black Prince said, "Lord Audley, the arms — and weapons — of death embrace us round, and comfort have we none except that in dying we pay in advance for a sweeter life.

"On the Crécy battlefield, our clouds of warlike cannon-smoke choked and smothered those French mouths and dispersed the French soldiers, but now their multitudes of millions hide the beauteous burning sun, as if it were behind a mask, leaving no hope to us but instead leaving sullen dark and the eyeless terror of all-ending night."

Lord Audley said, "This sudden, mighty, and quick headway that they have made, fair Prince, is wonderful. Before us in the valley lies King John II of France, with all the advantages that Heaven and earth can yield. His part of the French forces is stronger in the number of deployed troops than our whole army.

"His son Charles, the defiant Duke of Normandy, has arrayed the mountain on our right hand in shining plate armor, so that now the aspiring hill looks like a silver quarry, or an orb — the silvery moon. On the hill the banners, bannerets, and stretched-out-by-the-wind pendants often cuff the air and beat the winds that struggle to kiss them on account of their gaudiness.

"On our left hand lies Philip, the younger son of King John II, coating and covering the other hill in such array that all his gilded upright pikes seem to be straight trees of gold and the pendants seem to be leaves, and their device of ancient heraldry, quartered in colors suitable for sundry fruits, makes it the orchard of the Hesperides — the goddesses of the west.

"Behind us, too, the hill presents its height, for like a half-moon opening only one way, it rounds us in — there at our backs are lodged the fatal crossbows, and the army there is governed by the rough Chatillon.

"Then thus it stands: King John II has made secure for the French the valley we could use for our flight. The hills on either hand are proudly made royal by his royal sons. And on the hill behind us stands certain death — Death is in the pay of and provides service to Chatillon."

Edward the Black Prince said, "Death's name is much mightier than his deeds; your mentioning separately the parts of the military force of the French King has made it seem more than it is. These quarters, these squadrons, and these regiments, before us, behind us, and on either hand of us, are only one military force.

"When we name a man, his hand, his foot, and his head have individual strengths, but they are all one being with the strength of one self. Why, Lord Audley, all this many is only one, and we can call it all only one man's strength.

"He who has far to go counts the distance by miles. If he were to count the distance by steps, it would kill his heart and completely discourage him.

"The number of drops of water that make a flood is infinite, and yet you know we call it only a rain.

"As many sands as these my hands can hold are only my handful of so many sands; they are easily taken up and quickly thrown away. But if I stand to count them sand by sand, the number would confound and dumbfound my memory and make a thousand millions of a task that briefly is no more indeed than one: one handful of sand.

"There is only one France, and only one King of France: France has no more Kings than one, and that same King has only the powerful military force of one King.

"And we also have one powerful military force.

"So then fear no odds, for one to one is fair odds and fair equality."

A herald from King John II of France arrived.

Edward the Black Prince said, "What are your tidings, messenger? Speak plainly and briefly."

The French herald said, "King John II of France, my sovereign lord and master, through me greets his foe, the Prince of Wales. If you will call forth a hundred men of reputation — lords, knights, esquires, and English gentlemen — and if they and you will kneel at his feet, he immediately will fold his bloody battle flags, and ransom shall redeem your forfeited lives. If you will not, then this day shall drink more English blood than ever was buried in our Breton earth. What is the answer to his proffered mercy?"

Edward the Black Prince replied, "This Heaven that covers France contains the mercy that draws from me submissive prayers. May the Lord forbid that such base breath should vanish from my lips to urge the plea of mercy to a man.

"Return and tell your King that my tongue is made of steel, and it shall beg my mercy on his coward helmet. My tongue is my sword.

"Tell him my battle flags are as red as his, my men as bold, our English arms as strong. Return to him my defiance in his face."

"I go," the herald said.

A second French herald arrived, leading a jennet — a small Spanish horse.

Edward the Black Prince asked, "What message do you bring?"

The second French herald said, "Prince Charles Duke of Normandy, who is my lord and master, pitying your youth that is so surrounded with peril, by me has sent a nimble-jointed jennet, as swift as any yet you have bestrode, and he advises you to use it to flee, else Death himself has sworn that you shall die."

Edward the Black Prince asked, "Go back with the beast to the beast that sent it! Tell him I cannot sit on a coward's horse. Tell him to bestride the jade himself today, for I will stain my horse quite all over with blood and double gild my spurs with blood, but I will catch him."

A jade is a poor horse.

Edward the Black Prince continued, "So tell the capering dancing boy, and get yourself gone."

The second French herald exited, and a third French herald arrived. He was carrying a book of prayers.

The third French herald said, "Edward of Wales, Philip the younger son to the most mighty Christian King of France, seeing that your body's living date has expired, he, all full of charity and Christian love, hands over this book that is fully packed with prayers to your fair hand, and he entreats you that during your last remaining hour of life you meditate on the prayers therein and arm your soul for her long journey that is approaching.

"Thus have I done his bidding, and I return."

Edward the Black Prince said, "Herald of Philip, greet your lord from me. All good that he can send I can receive, but don't you think the foolhardy boy has wronged himself in thus far feeling concern for me?

"Perhaps he cannot pray without the book. I don't think he is an extempore clergyman. So then take back to him this compilation of prayers to do himself good in adversity.

"Besides, he doesn't know my sins' quality, and therefore he knows no prayers for my benefit.

"Before this night his prayer may be to pray to God to put it in my heart to hear his prayer — his prayer for me to be merciful to him.

"Tell the courtly wanton boy this, and go now."

The third French herald said, "I go."

Edward the Black Prince said, "How confident their strength and numbers makes them! Now, Lord Audley, sound those silver wings of yours and let those milk-white messengers of time show your time's learning in this dangerous time."

The silver wings were silver words, and the milk-white messengers of time were words that reflected the wisdom acquired by Lord Audley, who was older than the Black Prince and who had silvery white hair.

Edward the Black Prince said, "You yourself are constantly engaged in and scarred with many battles, and past stratagems are with iron pens — swords — written in the scars of your honorable face. You are a married — experienced — man in this distress, but danger woos me as it would woo a blushing maid. Teach me an answer to this perilous time. How should I respond when facing a dangerous battle of this kind?"

Lord Audley said, "To die is entirely as common as to live. The one in choice holds the other in chase. We choose one or the other, but whichever we choose, we then chase after the other. We may choose life, but we then continue on to death. If we choose death, we then continue on to the life that follows death.

"From the instant we begin to live, we pursue and hunt the time to die. First we bud, then we blossom, and afterward we mature and bear fruit, and then soon we fall, and just as a shade follows the body, so we follow death.

"If then we hunt for death, why do we fear it?

"If we fear death, why do we follow it?

"If we fear death, how can we shun it?

"If we fear death, then with fear we only aid the thing we fear to seize on us the sooner.

"Even if we don't fear death, still no determined effort can overthrow the fixed end and prescribed time of our fate, for whether we are ripe or rotten, we shall drop and die when we draw the lottery of our doom."

Edward the Black Prince said, "Ah, good old man, a thousand thousand armors these words of yours have buckled on my back.

"Ah, what an idiot you have shown life to be when it seeks the thing it fears; and how you have disgraced the imperial victory of murdering Death, since all the lives his conquering arrows strike seek him, and he does not seek them. This shames Death's glory.

"I will not give a penny for a life, nor half a halfpenny to shun grim death since to live is only to seek to die, and dying is only the beginning of new life.

"Let come the hour of my death when He Who rules it wishes it to come. I am indifferent whether I live or die."

<h1 style="text-align:center">— 4.5 —</h1>

<h1 style="text-align:center">[Scene 13]</h1>

King John II of France and his son Prince Charles Duke of Normandy talked together.

King John II of France said, "A sudden darkness has defaced the sky, the winds are gone, having crept into their caves because of fear, the leaves do not move, the world is hushed and still, the birds cease singing, and the wandering brooks murmur no accustomed greeting to their shores. Silence awaits some wonder, and expects that Heaven should pronounce some prophecy. Where or from whom proceeds this silence, Charles?"

Prince Charles Duke of Normandy replied, "Our men with open mouths and staring eyes look at each other, as if they await each other's words, and yet no creature speaks. A tongue-tied fear has made a midnight hour, and speeches sleep through all the waking regions."

King John II of France said, "Just now the splendid sun in all its pride looked through his golden coach upon the world, and suddenly it has hidden itself so that now the earth under the sun is like a grave: dark, deadly, silent, and comfortless."

Ravens cried.

King John II of France said, "Listen, what a deadly outcry I hear."

Prince Philip, his younger son, arrived.

Prince Charles Duke of Normandy said, "Here comes Philip, my brother."

"He is all dismayed," King John II of France said.

He then asked Prince Philip, "What fearful words are those that your looks presage?"

"A flight! A flight!" Prince Philip said.

King John II of France, immediately thinking of a flight of his soldiers, said, "Coward, what flight? You lie — there is no need for flight."

"A flight!" Prince Philip repeated.

King John II of France said, "Awaken your cowardly powers, and pull yourself together. Tell the substance of that complete fear indeed that is so ghastly printed in your face. What is the matter?"

Prince Philip said, "A flight of ugly ravens croak and hover over our soldiers' heads, and keep in triangles and cornered squares, imitating exactly those in which our forces are drawn up. With their approach there came this sudden fog, which now has hidden the airy flower of Heaven — the sun — and made at noon an unnatural night upon the quaking and dismayed world. In brief, our soldiers have let fall their weapons and stand like petrified images, bloodless and pale, each one gazing on another."

"Aye, now I call to mind the prophecy, but I must give no entrance to a fear," King John II of France said. "Return and put some heart in these yielding souls. Tell them that the ravens, seeing them in arms — so many fair French soldiers against a famished few English soldiers — have come simply to dine upon their handiwork and prey upon the carrion that they will kill. For when we see a horse lying down to die, although it is yet not dead, the ravenous birds sit watching and waiting for the departure of its life. Just like that, these ravens are waiting for the carcasses of those poor English soldiers who are marked to die. The ravens hover about, and if they cry to us it is only because of the meat that we must kill for them.

"Go now, and comfort my soldiers, and sound the trumpets, and at once deal with and end this little business of a foolish delusion."

Prince Philip exited.

The Earl of Salisbury arrived; he was the prisoner of a French Captain.

The French Captain said to King John II, "Behold, my liege, this knight and forty more knights — of whom the better part have been slain or have fled — with all endeavor sought to break our ranks and make their way to the surrounded Edward the Black Prince. Dispose of him as it pleases your majesty."

King John II of France ordered, "Go, and the next bough, soldier, that you see, hang him on it. Disgrace the bough with his body immediately. For I hold a tree in France too good to be the gallows of an English thief and therefore hanging an English thief on it is a disgrace to the tree."

The Earl of Salisbury said to Prince Charles Duke of Normandy, "My lord of Normandy, I have your passport and warrant for my safety as I ride through this land."

"Villiers procured it for you, didn't he?" Prince Charles Duke of Normandy asked.

"He did," the Earl of Salisbury answered.

"And it is current and valid," Prince Charles Duke of Normandy said. "You shall freely pass."

"Yes," King John II of France said to the Earl of Salisbury. "You shall pass freely to the gallows to be hanged, without denial or impediment."

He then ordered, "Take him away."

Prince Charles Duke of Normandy said, "I hope your highness will not so disgrace me and destroy the virtue of my seal at arms. He has my never-broken promise of safety to show, a passport signed by this Princely hand of mine, and it is better to let me cease to be a Prince than to break the firm pledge of a Prince. I earnestly beg you to let him pass through this territory peaceably and safely."

King John II of France said, "Both you and your word are in my command. What can you promise that I cannot break? Which of these two is the greater infamy: to disobey your father or to disobey yourself? Your word, and no man's word, may exceed the King's power.

"A man does not break his word as long as he keeps his word to the utmost of his power. The breach of faith dwells in the soul's consent; if you without your consent break your faith, you are not charged with the breach of faith."

He ordered, "Go and hang him, for your license to act lies in me, and my forcing you to do this is your excuse for doing it. My command exonerates you."

Prince Charles Duke of Normandy said, "Am I not a soldier in my word? Then arms, *adieu,* and let them fight who wish. Shall I not give away my belt from my waist only to have a guardian control me and tell me that I may not give my own things away?

"Upon my soul, if Edward Prince of Wales had given his word, written down in his noble handwriting, for all your knights to pass through the land of his father, then the royal King Edward III of England, to show favor to his warlike son, would not just give safe conduct to them, but would with all generosity have feasted them and theirs."

King John II of France replied, "Do you dwell on precedents, on worthy examples of chivalry? Then so be it."

He then asked the Earl of Salisbury, "Tell me, Englishman, what rank you are."

The Earl of Salisbury replied, "I am an Earl in England, although a prisoner here, and those who know me call me Earl of Salisbury."

King John II of France said, "Then, Earl of Salisbury, say where you are going."

"To Calais, where my liege, King Edward III, is," the Earl of Salisbury answered.

"To Calais, Earl of Salisbury?" King John II of France said. "Then to Calais be off, and tell King Edward III to prepare a noble grave in which to put his Princely son, black Edward.

"And as you travel westward from this place, some two leagues from here there is a lofty hill whose top seems topless, for the embracing sky hides the hill's high head in her blue, azured bosom.

"Upon the hill's tall top, when your foot reaches it, look back at the humble vale below — humble recently, but now made proud with arms — and there behold the wretched Prince of Wales hooped with a bond of iron round about him.

"After you see this sight, to Calais spur speedily and say that the massive numbers of his enemies smothered and suffocated the Black Prince with no need to slay him with a sword or arrow, and tell the King this is not all his trouble and ill, for I will greet him before he thinks I will.

"Away, be gone! Just the smoke of our shot will choke our foes, although bullets hit them not."

[Scene 14]

Edward the Black Prince and the Count of Artois talked together during the Battle of Poitiers.

The Count of Artois asked, "How fares your grace? Aren't you exhausted, my lord?"

"No, dear Count of Artois, I am not exhausted," Edward the Black Prince said, "but I am choked with dust and smoke, and so I stepped aside a moment for breath and fresher air."

"Breathe then and rest a moment, and then go to it again," the Count of Artois said. "The amazed French are quite distracted with gazing on the crows, and if our quivers were full of arrows again, your grace would see a glorious day of this."

He prayed, "Oh, for more arrows, Lord — that's our need."

"Have courage, Count of Artois," Edward the Black Prince said. "I wouldn't give a fig for feathered arrows when feathered fowls band together and fight on our side! What need have we to fight and sweat and keep making a fuss, when railing crows outscold our adversaries?"

Of course, he knew that they had to keep on fighting.

He said, "Up, up, Count of Artois! The ground itself is armed with fire-containing flint; command our archers to hurl away their variegated-in-color yew bows and go to battle with stones."

Sparks fly when flint and steel are struck together.

Edward the Black Prince continued, "Away, Count of Artois, away! My soul prophesies we will win the day."

Birds had frightened the French army, fulfilling this prophecy: "*feathered fowl shall make your army tremble.*"

The English archers began to fight with stones, fulfilling this prophecy: "*flintstones [shall] rise and break the battle array.*"

In another part of the battlefield, King John II of France said to himself, "Our multitudes are in themselves stunned, dismayed, and distraught with fear; swift-starting fear has buzzed — whispered — a cold dismay through all our army, and every petty disadvantage prompts the fear-possessed abject soul to flee. Even I, whose spirit is steel compared to their dull lead, what with recalling of the prophecy that stated that our native stones from English arms will rebel against us, find myself tainted with the strong surprise of weak and yielding fear."

Prince Charles Duke of Normandy arrived and said, "Flee, father, flee! The French kill the French: Some who would make a stand and fight let drive at some who flee. Our drums strike nothing but discouragement. Our trumpets sound dishonor and retreat. The spirit of fear that fears nothing but death — and does not fear dishonor — cowardly works confusion on itself."

Prince Philip arrived and said, "Pluck out your eyes, so you don't see this day's shame! An arm has beaten an army: one poor David has with a stone foiled twenty stout Goliaths. Some twenty naked starvelings with small stones of flint have driven back a powerful army of men arrayed and fortified in all military trappings."

"*Mort Dieu!*" King John II of France said. "They throw stones at us and kill us. No less than forty thousand wicked elders have this day been stoned to death by forty lean slaves."

Prince Charles Duke of Normandy said, "Oh, I wish that I were the citizen of some other country! This day has set derision on the French, and all the world will mock us and scorn us."

King John II of France asked, "Is there no hope left?"

"No hope but death to bury our shame," Prince Philip said.

"Move up to the front once more with me!" King John II of France said. "The twentieth part of those who live are men enough to make quail the feeble handful of the English."

"Then let us charge again," Prince Charles Duke of Normandy said. "If Heaven is not opposed to us, we cannot lose the day."

King John II of France said, "On! Away! Let's go!"

In another part of the battlefield, Lord Audley fought, but was wounded. Two esquires rescued him. An esquire is a young nobleman who is in training to be a knight.

"How fares my lord?" the first esquire asked. "How are you?"

Punning on "fare," Lord Audley replied, "I fare just as a man may do who dines at such a bloody feast as this."

"I hope, my lord, that is no mortal wound," the second esquire said.

Lord Audley replied, "It doesn't matter if it is, the account of my life is cast, and at the worst a mortal man dies.

"Good friends, convey me to the Princely Edward the Black Prince so that in the crimson bravery of my blood I may honor him by saluting him. I'll smile and tell him that this open wound ends the harvest of his Lord Audley's war."

— 4.7 —

[Scene 15]

The battle was over, and the English had won. Edward the Black Prince stood with two important prisoners: King John II of France and Prince Charles Duke of Normandy. Many battle flags were displayed, and some English soldiers were present. A French retreat sounded.

Edward the Black Prince said, "John in France, and lately John King of France, your bloody battle flags are now my captive colors, and both John and you, high vaunting Charles Duke of Normandy, who earlier today sent me a horse on which to flee, are now the subjects of my clemency.

"Ha, lords, isn't it a shame that English boys, whose early days are not yet worth a beard, should in the bosom of your Kingdom thus, one against twenty, beat both of you?"

King John II of France said, "Your fortune, not your military force, has conquered us."

Edward the Black Prince said, "That is an argument that Heaven has aided the side that is in the right."

The Count of Artois arrived, with Prince Philip as his prisoner.

Edward the Black Prince said, "See! See! The Count of Artois brings along with him the French Prince Philip who recently advised me about my soul.

"Welcome, Count of Artois, and welcome, Prince Philip, too.

"Prince Philip, who now, you or I, has a need to pray?

"Now is the proverb verified in you: Too bright a morning breeds a gloomy day."

Trumpets sounded. Lord Audley arrived, helped by the two esquires.

Edward the Black Prince said, "But say, what grim discouragement comes here? Alas, what thousand armed men of France have written that note of death in Lord Audley's face?

"Speak, Lord Audley, you who are wooing death with your carefree smile and are looking so merrily upon your grave as if you were in love with your death. What hungry sword has so devastated your face and lopped a true friend from my loving soul?"

81

Lord Audley said, "Oh, Prince, your sweet sorrowful speech to me is like a mournful knell to one who is deadly sick."

"Dear Lord Audley," Edward the Black Prince said, "if my tongue rings out your end, my arms shall be your grave. What may I do to win your life or to revenge your death? If you will drink the blood of captive Kings, or if such blood is restorative, order a round of drinks of Kings' blood, and I'll drink to you. If honor may gain exemption for you from death, take the whole share of the never-dying honor of this day, Lord Audley, for yourself and live."

Lord Audley said, "Victorious Prince, and to prove that you are so, behold a Caesar's fame in Kings' captivity — look at your Princely prisoners. If I could hold dim death at bay until after I saw my liege, your royal father, my soul with all willingness would then yield this castle of my flesh, this mangled tribute, to darkness, consummation, dust, and worms."

"Fortunately, bold man, your soul is all too proud to yield her city for one little breach, one little wound," Edward the Black Prince said. "Your soul is all too proud to be divorced from her earthly spouse by the soft temper of a Frenchman's sword.

"Listen, to repair your life I give to you three thousand marks a year in English land."

Lord Audley said, "I take your gift to pay the debts I owe. At the strong and dear risk of their lives, these two poor esquires rescued me from the French soldiers. What you have just given to me, I give to them, and as you love and respect me, Prince, give your consent to this bequest in my last testament."

"Renowned Lord Audley," Edward the Black Prince said, "live and have from me this gift doubled. These esquires shall have and you shall have three thousand marks a year in English land. But live or die, what you have given away to these and theirs shall be freely granted in perpetuity."

He then ordered, "Come, gentlemen, I will see my friend placed on a comfortable litter, and then we'll march proudly toward Calais at a triumphant pace to my royal father; and there bring the tribute of my wars: fair France's King."

CHAPTER 5
— 5.1 —
[Scene 16]

King Edward III, Queen Philippa, and the Earl of Derby talked together before Calais. Some English soldiers were present.

King Edward III said, "No more, Queen Philippa. Calm yourself. Copland, unless he can excuse his fault, shall find displeasure written in our looks.

"And now let me turn my attention to this proud resisting town: Soldiers, assault! I will no longer wait only to be deluded by their false delays. Put all inside Calais to the sword, and make the spoils your own."

Six citizens of Calais, wearing linen shirts, barefoot, and with halters about their necks, arrived, crying, "Mercy, King Edward III, mercy, gracious lord!"

"Contemptuous villains," King Edward III said, "do you call now for a truce? My ears are stopped against your fruitless cries."

He ordered his soldiers, "Sound drums' alarum! Draw threatening swords!"

"Ah, noble Prince, take pity on this town," the first citizen of Calais said, "and hear us, mighty King. We claim the promise that your highness made: The two days' respite you gave us is not yet expired, and we have come with willingness to bear whatever torturing death or punishment you please to give us in order that the trembling multitude inside Calais can be saved."

"My promise?" King Edward III said.

Earlier, he had said this: "I will accept nothing but fire and sword, unless, within these next two days, six of the men who are the wealthiest merchants in the town come to me entirely naked except for their linen shirts. Each rich merchant will wear a halter hung about his neck and will prostrate yield himself to me upon his knees to be afflicted, hanged, or whatever I please."

Remembering what he had said earlier, he now said, "Well, I do confess as much, but I require that the chiefest citizens and the men of most account should submit to me. You, perhaps, are only servile fellows, or some felonious robbers on the sea — pirates — whom, apprehended, the law would execute, even if we were to be merciful to you. No, no, you cannot outwit us in this way."

The second citizen of Calais said, "The sun, dread lord, that sets now in the west sees us brought low through misery. That same sun in the orient red of the morn saluted earlier our coming forth when we were men of reputation. If this is not true, may our afterlife be with the damned fiends in Hell."

"If what you said is true, then let our covenant stand," King Edward III said. "We take possession of the town in peace, but as for yourselves look for no pity. As imperial justice has decreed, your bodies shall be dragged around these walls of Calais, and afterwards you shall feel the stroke of steel as your bodies are cut into quarters. This is your punishment — go, soldiers, see to it that it is done."

Queen Philippa pleaded, "Ah, be milder to these yielding men. It is a glorious thing to establish peace, and Kings approach the nearest to God by giving life and safety to men.

"Since you intend to be King of France, let her people live to call you King, for what the sword cuts down or fire has spoiled is not held to be ours — dead subjects are no subjects."

King Edward III said, "Although experience teaches us that it is true that peaceful quietness brings most delight when most of all offenses are punished, yet in order that it shall be known that we can master our strong emotions as well as conquer others by the dint of sword, you shall prevail, Philippa; we yield to your request. These men shall live to boast of clemency. And, Tyranny, you can strike terror to yourself. Let tyrants fear inevitable retribution."

The six citizens of Calais shouted, "Long live your highness, and happy be your reign!"

"Go, get you hence," King Edward III said. "Return to the town, and if this kindness has deserved your love, learn then to revere Edward III as your King."

The six citizens of Calais exited.

King Edward III said, "Now might we hear of our affairs abroad. We would, until gloomy winter were at an end, place our men in garrison for a while."

Seeing some people coming, he asked, "But who comes here?"

John Copland and his prisoner, King David II of Scotland, arrived.

The Earl of Derby said, "This is John Copland, my lord, and David II — the King of Scots."

King Edward III asked, "Is this the proud presumptuous esquire of the North who would not yield his prisoner to my Queen?"

"I am, my liege, a northern esquire indeed," John Copland replied, "but I trust that I am neither proud nor insolent."

"What moved you then to be so obstinate as to contradict our royal Queen's desire?" King Edward III asked.

"No willful disobedience, mighty lord," John Copland said, "but my desert and accepted code of warfare. I captured the King of Scotland myself in single fight and like a soldier I would be loath to lose the least pre-eminence that I had won.

"I, Copland, immediately upon your highness' order have come to France, and with a lowly mind I submit to you the fruit of my victory. Receive, dread lord, the customary tribute of my freight that I have sailed across the channel. Here is the wealthy tribute of my laboring hands, a King who would long since have been surrendered if only your gracious self had been in London."

Queen Philippa objected, "But, Copland, you scorned the King's command when you neglected our commission in his name. King Edward III delegated his authority to me."

John Copland replied, "The King's name I revere, but I revere his person more. His name shall keep me in allegiance always, but to his person I will bend my knee."

King Edward III said to his Queen, "I ask you, Philippa, let your displeasure pass: This man pleases me, and I like his words. For what is a man who will attempt great deeds and lose the glory that ensues from those deeds? All rivers flow into the sea, and Copland's allegiance has the same relation to his King."

He ordered John Copland, "Kneel down."

He then dubbed Copland's shoulders with a sword and said, "Now rise as King Edward III's knight. To maintain your new position as a knight, I give five hundred marks a year in absolute possession to you and yours."

Sir John Copland stood up.

The Earl of Salisbury arrived.

King Edward III said, "Welcome, Lord Salisbury — what news do you bring from Bretagne?"

"This, mighty King," the Earl of Salisbury said. "The country we have won, and Charles de Lord Mountfort, regent of that place, presents your highness with this coronet, protesting true allegiance to your grace."

He gave the coronet to the King.

King Edward III said, "We thank you for your service, valiant Earl. Demand as a right our favor, for we owe it to you."

The Earl of Salisbury said, "This was joyful news, but now, my lord, my voice must be tragic and I must sing of doleful incidents."

King Edward III asked, "Have our men been overthrown at Poitiers? Or is our son beset with too great odds?"

The Earl of Salisbury said, "Edward the Black Prince was beset by too great odds. As my worthless self with forty other loyal knights, under the safe conduct of the Dauphin's seal travelled that way, finding him distressed, a troop of lancers met us on the way, surprised us, and brought us as prisoners to King John II, who, proud of this and eager of revenge, commanded that all our heads immediately be cut off.

"And we surely would have died except that Prince Charles Duke of Normandy, who was more full of honor than his angry father, procured our quick deliverance from thence. But before we went, King John II said, 'Salute your King. Tell him to provide a funeral for his son. Today our sword shall cut his thread of life, and sooner than Edward III thinks we'll be with him to repay those injuries he has done to us.'

"This said, we passed, not daring to reply. Our hearts were dead, our looks troubled and wan. Wandering, at last we climbed a hill from whence, although our grief had been much before, yet now seeing the state of affairs did three times as much increase our sorrow, for there, my lord, oh, there we saw down in a valley how both armies lay.

"The French had cast their trenches like a ring, and all the holes in the barricades were thickly embossed with brass cannon.

"Here stood a battalion of ten thousand cavalry, and there stood twice as many pike-wielding soldiers in a square formation.

"Here were crossbows and deadly wounding arrows, and in the midst — like a slender point within the compass of the horizon, like a rising bubble in the sea, like a hazel wand in a wood of pines, or like a bear firmly chained to a stake — stood famous Edward the Black Prince, always awaiting the time when those dogs of France would fasten on his flesh.

"Soon the death-procuring knell began. Off went the cannons that with trembling noise shook the very mountain where they stood. Then sounded the trumpets' clangor in the air. The armies joined in battle, and when we could no longer discern the difference between the friend and the foe, so intricate was the dark confusion, we turned our watery eyes away with sighs as black as powder fuming into smoke, and thus, I, unhappy, fear that I have told the most untimely tale of Edward the Black Prince's fall."

Queen Philippa mourned, "Ah, me, is this my welcome into France? Is this the comfort that I looked to have when I would meet with my beloved son? Sweet Ned, I wish that your mother would have drowned in the sea so that she would not now experience this mortal grief."

King Edward III said, "Calm yourself, Philippa. Tears will not serve to call him back if he has been taken away. Comfort yourself as I do, gentle Queen, with hope of sharp, unheard-of, dire revenge. King John II of France tells me to provide a funeral for my son! And so I will, but all the peers in France shall be mourners, and they shall weep bloody tears until their empty veins become dry and parched. The pillars of his hearse shall be their bones, the soil that covers him shall be the ashes of their city, his knell shall be the groaning cries of dying men, and instead of candles on his tomb, a hundred and fifty towers shall burning blaze while we wail for our valiant son's decease."

A trumpet sounded, and a herald arrived and said, "Rejoice, my lord, and ascend the imperial throne of France! The mighty and feared Prince of Wales, great soldier in arms to the bloody god of war, Mars, and the Frenchman's terror and England's fame, rides triumphant like a Roman peer, and, lowly at his stirrup, comes on foot King John II of France, together with his son in captive bonds, whose diadem Edward the Black Prince brings to crown you with and to proclaim you King."

King Edward III said, "Stop mourning, Philippa, and wipe your eyes. Let trumpets sound and welcome in Plantagenet!"

Edward the Black Prince, King John II of France, Prince Philip, Lord Audley, and the Count of Artois arrived.

King Edward III said, "As things long lost when they are found again, so does my son make his father's heart rejoice, for whom just now my soul was much troubled."

Queen Philippa said, "Let this be a token to express my joy" — she kissed him — "for inward passions will not let me speak."

Edward the Black Prince gave King Edward III the French crown and said, "My gracious father, here receive this gift, this wreath of conquest and reward of war, got with as great peril of our lives as ever was a thing of price before this day. Install your highness in your proper right, and here also I render to your hands these prisoners, who were the chief cause of our strife."

"So, John of France, I see that you keep your word," King Edward III said. "You promised to be sooner with ourself than we did think you would be, and it is so indeed. But if you had done at first as now you do, how many civilized towns had stood untouched that now are turned to broken heaps of stones? How many people's lives might you have saved who are prematurely sunken into their graves?"

"Edward, don't recount irrevocable things," King John II of France said. "Tell me what ransom you require from me."

"Your ransom, John, hereafter shall be known," King Edward III said, "but first you must cross the seas to see what entertainment England affords. However it falls out, it cannot be as bad as ours has been since we arrived in France."

"Accursed man!" King John II of France said. "Of this I was foretold, but I misinterpreted what the prophet foretold."

This was the prophecy:

"*Yet in the end your foot you shall advance,*

"*As far in England as your foe in France.*"

"Now, father," Edward the Black Prince said, "this petition Edward makes to you, whose grace has been his strongest shield: That as your pleasure chose me for the man to be the instrument to show your power, so you will grant that many Princes more, bred and brought up within that little isle, may constantly be famous for similar victories.

"And as for my part, the bloody scars that I bear, the weary nights that I have stayed awake and watched in the field, the dangerous conflicts that I have often had, the fearful menaces that were offered to me, the heat and cold, and whatever else might displease, I wish were now redoubled twentyfold, so that later ages, when they read about the painful events of my tender youth, might thereby be inflamed with such resolve as not the territories of France alone, but likewise Spain, Turkey, and whatever countries else that would provoke fair England's just ire, might at their presence tremble and retire."

"Here, English lords, we proclaim a rest, an intermission of our painful arms," King Edward III said. "Sheath your swords, refresh your weary limbs, peruse your spoils, and after we have breathed a day or two within this haven town, God willing, then we'll ship for England, where in a happy hour I trust we — three Kings (Edward III, John II, and David II), two princes (Edward and Philip), and a Queen (Philippa) — shall arrive."

APPENDIX A: ABOUT THE AUTHOR

It was a dark and stormy night. Suddenly a cry rang out, and on a hot summer night in 1954, Josephine, wife of Carl Bruce, gave birth to a boy — me. Unfortunately, this young married couple allowed Reuben Saturday, Josephine's brother, to name their first-born. Reuben, aka "The Joker," decided that Bruce was a nice name, so he decided to name me Bruce Bruce. I have gone by my middle name — David — ever since.

Being named Bruce David Bruce hasn't been all bad. Bank tellers remember me very quickly, so I don't often have to show an ID. It can be fun in charades, also. When I was a counselor as a teenager at Camp Echoing Hills in Warsaw, Ohio, a fellow counselor gave the signs for "sounds like" and "two words," then she pointed to a bruise on her leg twice. Bruise Bruise? Oh yeah, Bruce Bruce is the answer!

Uncle Reuben, by the way, gave me a haircut when I was in kindergarten. He cut my hair short and shaved a small bald spot on the back of my head. My mother wouldn't let me go to school until the bald spot grew out again.

Of all my brothers and sisters (six in all), I am the only transplant to Athens, Ohio. I was born in Newark, Ohio, and have lived all around Southeastern Ohio. However, I moved to Athens to go to Ohio University and have never left.

At Ohio U, I never could make up my mind whether to major in English or Philosophy, so I got a bachelor's degree with a double major in both areas, then I added a Master of Arts degree in English and a Master of Arts degree in Philosophy. Yes, I have my MAMA degree.

Currently, and for a long time to come (I eat fruits and veggies), I am spending my retirement writing books such as *Nadia Comaneci: Perfect 10*, *The Funniest People in Comedy*, *Homer's* Iliad: *A Retelling in Prose*, and *William Shakespeare's* Hamlet: *A Retelling in Prose*.

If all goes well, I will publish one or two books a year for the rest of my life. (On the other hand, a good way to make God laugh is to tell Her your plans.)

By the way, my sister Brenda Kennedy writes romances such as *A New Beginning* and *Shattered Dreams*.

APPENDIX B: SOME BOOKS BY DAVID BRUCE

Retellings of a Classic Work of Literature

Arden of Faversham: *A Retelling*

Ben Jonson's The Alchemist: *A Retelling*

Ben Jonson's The Arraignment, or Poetaster: *A Retelling*

Ben Jonson's Bartholomew Fair: *A Retelling*

Ben Jonson's The Case is Altered: *A Retelling*

Ben Jonson's Catiline's Conspiracy: *A Retelling*

Ben Jonson's The Devil is an Ass: *A Retelling*

Ben Jonson's Epicene: *A Retelling*

Ben Jonson's Every Man in His Humor: *A Retelling*

Ben Jonson's Every Man Out of His Humor: *A Retelling*

Ben Jonson's The Fountain of Self-Love, or Cynthia's Revels: *A Retelling*

Ben Jonson's The Magnetic Lady, or Humors Reconciled: *A Retelling*

Ben Jonson's The New Inn, or The Light Heart: *A Retelling*

Ben Jonson's Sejanus' Fall: *A Retelling*

Ben Jonson's The Staple of News: *A Retelling*

Ben Jonson's A Tale of a Tub: *A Retelling*

Ben Jonson's Volpone, or the Fox: *A Retelling*

Christopher Marlowe's Complete Plays: Retellings

Christopher Marlowe's Dido, Queen of Carthage: *A Retelling*

Christopher Marlowe's Doctor Faustus: *Retellings of the 1604 A-Text and of the 1616 B-Text*

Christopher Marlowe's Edward II: *A Retelling*

Christopher Marlowe's The Massacre at Paris: *A Retelling*

Christopher Marlowe's The Rich Jew of Malta: *A Retelling*

Christopher Marlowe's Tamburlaine, Parts 1 and 2: *Retellings*

Dante's Divine Comedy: *A Retelling in Prose*

Dante's Inferno: *A Retelling in Prose*

Dante's Purgatory: *A Retelling in Prose*

Dante's Paradise: *A Retelling in Prose*

The Famous Victories of Henry V: *A Retelling*

From the Iliad *to the* Odyssey: *A Retelling in Prose of Quintus of Smyrna's* Posthomerica

George Chapman, Ben Jonson, and John Marston's Eastward Ho! *A Retelling*

George Peele's The Arraignment of Paris: *A Retelling*

George Peele's The Battle of Alcazar: *A Retelling*

George's Peele's David and Bathsheba, and the Tragedy of Absalom: *A Retelling*

George Peele's Edward I: *A Retelling*

George Peele's The Old Wives' Tale: *A Retelling*

George-a-Greene: *A Retelling*

The History of King Leir: *A Retelling*

Homer's Iliad: *A Retelling in Prose*

Homer's Odyssey: *A Retelling in Prose*

J.W. Gent.'s The Valiant Scot: *A Retelling*

Jason and the Argonauts: A Retelling in Prose of Apollonius of Rhodes' Argonautica

John Ford: Eight Plays Translated into Modern English

John Ford's The Broken Heart: *A Retelling*

John Ford's The Fancies, Chaste and Noble: *A Retelling*

John Ford's The Lady's Trial: *A Retelling*

John Ford's The Lover's Melancholy: *A Retelling*

John Ford's Love's Sacrifice: *A Retelling*

John Ford's Perkin Warbeck: *A Retelling*

John Ford's The Queen: *A Retelling*

John Ford's 'Tis Pity She's a Whore: *A Retelling*

John Lyly's Campaspe: *A Retelling*

John Lyly's Endymion, The Man in the Moon: *A Retelling*

John Lyly's Galatea: *A Retelling*

John Lyly's Love's Metamorphosis: *A Retelling*

John Lyly's Midas: *A Retelling*

John Lyly's Mother Bombie: *A Retelling*

John Lyly's Sappho and Phao: *A Retelling*

John Lyly's The Woman in the Moon: *A Retelling*

John Webster's The White Devil: *A Retelling*

King Edward III: *A Retelling*

Mankind: *A Medieval Morality Play* (A Retelling)

Margaret Cavendish's The Unnatural Tragedy: *A Retelling*

The Merry Devil of Edmonton: *A Retelling*

The Summoning of Everyman: *A Medieval Morality Play* (A Retelling)

Robert Greene's Friar Bacon and Friar Bungay: *A Retelling*

The Taming of a Shrew: *A Retelling*

Tarlton's Jests: A Retelling

Thomas Middleton's A Chaste Maid in Cheapside: *A Retelling*

Thomas Middleton's Women Beware Women: *A Retelling*

Thomas Middleton and Thomas Dekker's The Roaring Girl: *A Retelling*

Thomas Middleton and William Rowley's The Changeling: *A Retelling*

The Trojan War and Its Aftermath: Four Ancient Epic Poems

Virgil's Aeneid: *A Retelling in Prose*

William Shakespeare's 5 Late Romances: Retellings in Prose

William Shakespeare's 10 Histories: Retellings in Prose

William Shakespeare's 11 Tragedies: Retellings in Prose

William Shakespeare's 12 Comedies: Retellings in Prose

William Shakespeare's 38 Plays: Retellings in Prose
William Shakespeare's 1 Henry IV, aka Henry IV, Part 1: *A Retelling in Prose*
William Shakespeare's 2 Henry IV, aka Henry IV, Part 2: *A Retelling in Prose*
William Shakespeare's 1 Henry VI, aka Henry VI, Part 1: *A Retelling in Prose*
William Shakespeare's 2 Henry VI, aka Henry VI, Part 2: *A Retelling in Prose*
William Shakespeare's 3 Henry VI, aka Henry VI, Part 3: *A Retelling in Prose*
William Shakespeare's All's Well that Ends Well: *A Retelling in Prose*
William Shakespeare's Antony and Cleopatra: *A Retelling in Prose*
William Shakespeare's As You Like It: *A Retelling in Prose*
William Shakespeare's The Comedy of Errors: *A Retelling in Prose*
William Shakespeare's Coriolanus: *A Retelling in Prose*
William Shakespeare's Cymbeline: *A Retelling in Prose*
William Shakespeare's Hamlet: *A Retelling in Prose*
William Shakespeare's Henry V: *A Retelling in Prose*
William Shakespeare's Henry VIII: *A Retelling in Prose*
William Shakespeare's Julius Caesar: *A Retelling in Prose*
William Shakespeare's King John: *A Retelling in Prose*
William Shakespeare's King Lear: *A Retelling in Prose*
William Shakespeare's Love's Labor's Lost: *A Retelling in Prose*
William Shakespeare's Macbeth: *A Retelling in Prose*
William Shakespeare's Measure for Measure: *A Retelling in Prose*
William Shakespeare's The Merchant of Venice: *A Retelling in Prose*
William Shakespeare's The Merry Wives of Windsor: *A Retelling in Prose*
William Shakespeare's A Midsummer Night's Dream: *A Retelling in Prose*
William Shakespeare's Much Ado About Nothing: *A Retelling in Prose*
William Shakespeare's Othello: *A Retelling in Prose*
William Shakespeare's Pericles, Prince of Tyre: *A Retelling in Prose*
William Shakespeare's Richard II: *A Retelling in Prose*
William Shakespeare's Richard III: *A Retelling in Prose*
William Shakespeare's Romeo and Juliet: *A Retelling in Prose*
William Shakespeare's The Taming of the Shrew: *A Retelling in Prose*
William Shakespeare's The Tempest: *A Retelling in Prose*
William Shakespeare's Timon of Athens: *A Retelling in Prose*
William Shakespeare's Titus Andronicus: *A Retelling in Prose*
William Shakespeare's Troilus and Cressida: *A Retelling in Prose*
William Shakespeare's Twelfth Night: *A Retelling in Prose*
William Shakespeare's The Two Gentlemen of Verona: A Retelling in Prose
William Shakespeare's The Two Noble Kinsmen: *A Retelling in Prose*
William Shakespeare's The Winter's Tale: *A Retelling in Prose*